Oil & Water

A Brother's Best Friend Romance
Indie Sparks

Twice Shy Publishing

For every family misfit who simply couldn't conform, even if you'd wanted to, which you didn't, of course. I hope you've had your fair share of fun secrets along the way, and I wish you many more to come.

Contents

There's no Better Fit Than a Couple of Misfits

Sometimes, when he grows up to have a great beard,
challenging smirk, big firm hands, loyal heart, filthy mouth,
and a sixth sense when it comes to her needs,
a girl's just gotta do . . .
her brother's best friend.

Poolside Musings
Ellis

I'VE NEVER UNDERSTOOD THE need for a rehearsal dinner. This is my third one, and even with all the extras that my future sister-in-law has insisted on incorporating into her and my brother's wedding ceremony, there was no need to rehearse any of it.

At least that part of the evening is over. We all survived the performative remedial bullshit of proving we understood who to walk with and where to stand and when to turn and how to exit. A-B-C, 1-2-3, kiss-my-ass.

Right now, I am supposed to be inside the country club's dining room, moving of my own accord, mingling with the other captives of the wedding party and family members while waiting for dinner to be served instead of standing next to this beautiful sparkling pool, wishing I could dive into it and rehearse what really matters.

My opportunity to audition with the Fantasia Faeries Pod could come up at any time. I know I'm on their radar, and rumor has it that Shaydyn is considering retirement. If that's true, they'll be left without a green merfaery. And green is my signature color. I already have the right color tail, so that would have to be a point in my favor. Plus, I can hold my breath for the required three minutes, and I have a good tank presence. I can play to a crowd; I just need the opportunity to be in front of one.

Of course, I, of all people, know to take rumors with a grain of salt, having been rumored to be a mafia princess in high school. The Irish Mafia, to be clear.

In all fairness, my mother is of Irish descent, but Nora French is a pediatrician who wears Disney scrubs. Her family came to America by way of her immigrant great-grandparents who had been a maid and a sheep shearer in Donegal. My father is a research meteorologist whose family tree bears fruit from half the globe, but not a single leaf represents Ireland.

My parents are scientists, not gangsters.

Honestly, I'm still pretty sure my brother started the rumor that we were part of the Irish Mob. Brody's always been persuasive. I know for a fact he's the one who convinced Cody Jackson I was born with a tail to keep him from asking me to my eighth-grade dance.

Ironic to think that I cried for six hours straight back then over people believing I was born with a tail, and now I willingly wear one every chance I get. A tail I paid over three grand for.

Correction, am *still paying* for.

If you ask my mother what I do for a living, she will say I'm an esthetician. She likes the nearly medical ring of it. My father tells people I'm a makeup artist, said with a thinly-camouflaged hint of disdain in his voice.

They're both correct. I do work in a spa part-time, providing skincare services, and I also do makeup for weddings and the occasional film or photography shoot, but I'm also a professional mermaid.

My parents call that my hobby, say it's a phase, that I do it for the kids. I have always had a flare for the dramatic, after all.

But being a mermaid is a real job. I'm not just playing dress up.

I train hard, and I get paid to put on my tail and perform. That's the very definition of a job: you get paid to do it!

One day, I will be a member of the Fantasia Faeries, and I'll get paid to put on my tail and a luminous pair of waterproof wings, too. I'll entertain in professionally-maintained aquariums, no more kiddie parties in private pools.

Actually, those aren't the worst.

My worst gig so far was a bachelor party. Never. Again. The tips alone covered two payments on my tail, but for sunburned tits, I should've been able to pay the damn thing off. Thank Neptune for shell-shaped pasties because I don't think I could've survived sunburned nips.

I used sunscreen, I swear. But part Irish and with the reddish hair and fair skin, you know?

I'd hate to see my parents' faces if they heard about that day. Or my brother's, for that matter. On second thought, he'd deserve it for telling anyone I had a tail to begin with. Whoops! Guess what? She's got a tail and tits now. Let him be the uncomfortable one for a change.

Anyway, it's not like I was the first professional mermaid to be seen with bare breasts. Mermaid burlesque shows are a thing. And if I choose to do that someday, I won't care what anyone thinks about it.

When I put on my mermaid makeup and my shimmering tail, I become Ellisandra. Yes, my real name is Ellis, so maybe it's not the most original mermaid name I could've come up with. But it's one I'll remember and always be quick to answer to, and that matters when you're working with kids.

And beyond the kiddie shows, I think it sounds a little exotic. Alluring. Intriguing.

I just want to stand out. I want to be memorable. I *waaaaaaant—*

Anyone But Her
Malcolm

I SHOULDN'T BE GLUED to this window, staring at the shapely body illuminated only by the lights in the pool. She's been standing there since before I started standing here, and I can't look away. Damn, those curves in that dress.

My dick would like to make her acquaintance, but my date might still show, and if I'm outside chatting up another woman, she will undoubtedly make a scene. And that's the last thing I need tonight.

How do I know so much about my very late date's temperament? She's my ex-girlfriend. Many times over. Maybe I'm a slow learner. Maybe I'm just slow to let go of familiarity. Fine, I don't like change.

I date other women when Celeste and I are broken up, but when she comes back around, saying we should try again, I always go along with it. The last few times, though, I haven't really wanted to try again. But I agreed, anyway, because that's what I do.

She wouldn't let me pick her up tonight, insisting that since she isn't part of the wedding, it would be too awkward for her to be here during the actual rehearsal. I offered to leave after that part to come get her, but she refused. She also promised to be here on time to join us for dinner.

I confirmed a plus-one. But here I stand, minus one. And wishing I could go outside and talk to the one by the pool.

No can do, though. It's bad enough I'm probably going to be responsible for a wasted plate of prime rib. I can't risk being the evening's entertainment when my ex shoves me and the poor unsuspecting goddess who's wearing the hell out of that little black dress into the pool.

My whiskey glass sweats in my hand. It's not my first drink of the night, but I'm not drunk. Not yet.

I'm the best man. I've known French since we were in the sixth grade. Brody French, but he's one of those guys who got called by his last name outside of athletics. Everybody knew French. Star athlete, top of our class, all the girls loved him, enough charm to get him out of anything. And to make it even worse, he's actually a good guy. Impossible not to like.

And for some reason, he liked me. We clicked, became fast friends. His family became my second family . . . or my first, really. His mom treated me like another son. His sister was just as annoyed by me as she was her own brother.

His dad? Well, I think I threw off the balance in his perfect family, but he tolerated me. At times, he was great to me, taught me a lot about money and investing, things no one else was going to teach me. And he answered my endless questions about his job without telling me to shut up or making me feel stupid.

He made me realize it was okay to be interested in things my family didn't understand. I probably wouldn't be where I am today without him, but Gary French isn't what you'd call a fun guy. He's a scientist. Always.

His son was one of the biggest pranksters I'd ever met, but around his dad, Brody knew how to rein it in. I never did.

Unfortunately, I was the guy who always took the joke too far, never knew when to be serious. But that's the thing, I really didn't know. I wasn't trying to be obnoxious. I just didn't understand why some things were only funny in certain settings, why the same jokes or pranks could be acceptable in front of some people, but not others.

No one had ever taught me how to adjust my behavior according to the situation, so I mostly didn't. And Gary French couldn't understand how a kid as smart as I was could be such an idiot sometimes.

He was never crazy about the fact that his son had chosen me for a best friend, but at the same time, I think the guy felt sorry for me, at least enough to try to teach me how to navigate the world around me. There must've been times when he wondered how the hell I was going to survive as an adult.

I'm not only surviving. I'm thriving. I am at the top of my game, but my game is olive oil, and being an olive oil broker isn't a career choice a man like Gary French can wrap his head around.

He likens it to trading cryptocurrency or being a professional gambler. There are similarities, I guess. There's a lot of market analysis and forecasting involved, but it's not all guesswork and luck. That would be a losing argument with him, though.

For a weather researcher, you'd think he'd be more receptive to the similarities in our careers. Maybe he would be if I had the guts to point them out, but it's easier to just avoid the confrontation. And like I said, I kind of feel like I owe the guy, no matter how he dismisses my accomplishments.

I've never even mentioned that I'm also a certified olive oil taster.

At any rate, the last thing I want to do is ruin an important French family event.

Fuck it. I don't think Celeste is coming. I am a grown man, and I'm single. There is no reason I shouldn't walk out there and strike up a conversation with the woman by the pool.

She tilts her head to one side and then the other like she's cracking her neck. And then she reaches her hand behind her neck, extending it toward her opposite side and dragging her hair back from in front of her shoulder. With both hands, she lifts it and lets it fall. Damn, it's long. I thought she had short hair, but it was just all pulled to the front. She shakes her head now, and her long hair flows over her back.

Fuck me.

Damn, does she cut a striking profile when she turns to the side and looks up at the stars. I peel my gaze from the rounded silhouette of her breasts, letting it roam up her neck to her face.

Her face.

No. No, no, no, no, no . . . anyone but her.

Please.

Why? Why does she have to be Ellis French? I can't have a hard-on for Ellis! Shit. How have I been standing here, ogling my best friend's little sister all this time without recognizing her?

Brody would kill me. His dad would kill me. Hell, Ellis might kill me.

Why is my dick still throbbing against my zipper as if death might be worth it?

Stop it. Stop thinking of her as a woman. She's Ellis, your best friend's annoying little sister. Think of her like you did when you were growing up. You have to treat her like a kid sister, just like you always did. But she's standing out there with so much moon-kissed skin exposed . . . that body and that hair . . . there's only one way to fix this.

I open the door and I go. As fast as I can I go to her . . .

And I don't slow down until we hit the water.

Because this is exactly what I would've done when we were growing up.

Her eyes are open and staring directly into mine under the water. Maybe I should've stood at the window for just a beat longer, long enough to process one more thought before I acted, but I willed myself to think like teen Malcolm used to think, so I did what teen me would've done.

And now, she's about to do what teen Ellis would've done.

Looks like I'm making a scene at this rehearsal dinner after all.

Hopelessly Concussed
Ellis

I BREAK THE SURFACE with a fistful of Malcolm's hair in my right hand. Said hair is still attached to his head. His stupid, stupid head!

"What the hell is wrong with you?"

He sputters, and water dribbles from his mouth. I shove his face back under. When I yank him up again, I ask a simpler question. "Why?"

His eyes blink rapidly as he gasps for air, but no words come out of his mouth.

"You better start talking, Malcolm!"

"It was an accident."

"That was no fucking accident. You clotheslined me!" I shove his head under again.

He overpowers me this time and brings his head back above water. "I did not clothesline you. I wrapped you up by your waist. That was a totally safe tackle."

"Why did you tackle me? What were you thinking?"

His eyes fly wide, but his mouth stays shut.

"Answer me!"

"I-I wasn't thinking anything, I swear!"

"You shit-for-brains asshole. How am I supposed to go inside for dinner like this?"

"You're not the only one who's wet."

"I don't care about you being soaked. You're the one who caused this!"

"Okay. Stop yelling. I have towels in my trunk."

"Why? What are you, a serial killer?"

"Why would a serial killer have towels in his trunk?"

"Why would someone who isn't a serial killer have towels in his trunk?"

"Jesus, I forgot how weird you are. Let's go to my car before people notice us out here."

I swim to the shallow end and wade to the stairs, snatching the shoe I lost in the attack from the water as it floats by. "Sure, I'm the weird one. You freak."

"I should've realized I didn't need to knock you into the pool to kill my erection. I could've just come out here and talked to you for thirty seconds."

"Don't talk to me about your dick. God, how are you still so inappropriate?"

"I'm not. Usually. I can't help it if you tricked me into thinking you were someone else."

We glare at each other, both dripping onto the pool deck. "I didn't trick you into anything. I was out here minding my own business when you rammed into me."

"Let's not use that phrase to describe it."

"You're disgusting." I slip my other shoe off and start walking toward the parking lot. Malcolm trails behind me, saying nothing, which is probably in his best interest at this point.

He pops open his trunk, and sure enough, there's a basket holding a stack of folded towels. And a stack of folded t-shirts. "Did you come straight here from the laundromat?"

"No. I don't need to go to the laundromat; I own a washer and dryer. But I prefer to pay someone else to do my laundry. Lucky for us, I hadn't taken these inside yet."

I take the towel he's offering me and begin to wring out my drenched hair. "It never occurred to you that you could pay someone to come to your place and do your laundry?"

"The lady I take it to does a good job. Besides, I don't like strangers in my house."

It's no use trying to dry my body while wearing a wet dress, but I towel off my face and my arms. "I can't get dry like this. I'll just redo my makeup in my car and put my hair up. Maybe I can stand outside long enough for my dress to air dry. It's pretty thin material."

"It's very thin material." He gulps. "But you can't stay outside long enough for it to dry, and you absolutely cannot go back inside wearing that thin black dress while it's still wet. It's . . . clingy."

"Shit. I'm never going to hear the end of not being in my seat when dinner is served. But thanks to you, I have no choice. I'll drive like a maniac and hope for the best. This dress is green, by the way."

"Huh, it looked black through the window."

"It's night time, moron. Everything looks black in the dark. My dress is green. Green is my signature color, remember?"

"Yeah, I'm not sure I ever knew that."

"How could you not have known that?" A breeze rustles the pampas grass at the edge of the courtyard, casting shadows over the landscaping lights that create the illusion of flickering candles. I shiver as the evening air resettles around us.

"Take your dress off and wrap up in a towel. You can't drive home like that. You'll ruin your car seat."

"I'm not driving home in a towel."

"You can wear one of my t-shirts. It'll be so long on you that it'll look like a dress."

"That's maybe not a bad idea."

He undoes his belt, and then he starts unbuttoning his shirt.

"What are you doing?"

"I'm changing, too." He pulls a pair of shorts from under the stack of t-shirts and waves them at me like a matador waving a flag at a bull.

"Oh, right. Well, turn around. I'm not getting naked in front of you."

With our backs to each other, we undress at the edge of the dark parking lot with ancient oak branches blocking the stars. It's way darker out here than it was by the pool, or even by the pampas grass in the courtyard.

I'm sure my wet dress left nothing to his imagination, but I still don't want to stand in front of him naked and confirm his mind's image.

I lay my dress on his bumper and shimmy out of my underwear, setting them on top of my dress while I grab a fresh towel to dry my body. I'm bent over, drying my legs when a car careens through the side entrance of the lot and flies up behind us, slamming on the brakes and spotlighting my nakedness.

Who is arriving this late? Did they have to park right there? And why haven't they turned off their fucking headlights? Perv! I quickly wrap the towel around my body, and look up just in time to be blinded by their high beams switching on.

I can't see anything, but I clearly hear Malcolm's voice as he asks, "Can this night get any worse?"

And then I hear a car door slam and a woman's voice. "You fucking asshole! You cheating piece of shit asshole! You fucked Ellis French? In the parking lot? Seriously?"

Oh, shit. It's Celeste, Malcolm's lifelong girlfriend. Great. "We did not fuck!" I yell. "Not tonight, not ever. Not in this parking lot, not anywhere. Turn your goddamn headlights off!"

The world goes dark again. I blink as my eyes adjust. All I can see is spots. "Can you please hand me a t-shirt? I'll put it on in my car."

Soft cotton hits my palm, and I close my fingers around it. I use the towel I dried my hair with to gather my dress and my underwear. "I'll get these towels back to you."

Bending down again, I hook my fingers into the ankle straps of my shoes and walk away, leaving Malcolm to deal with Celeste. She's his problem, not mine.

I make it back to the club just in time to slide into my seat two seconds before my plate is set in front of me. I missed the salad, but I'm right on time for what was supposed to be fish. It's the prime rib instead, but seeing as how I'm late, I decide not to call any additional attention to myself.

Less than a minute later, Malcolm and Celeste take their seats. I hear her fake attempt to whisper—to be honest, everyone probably hears her—that she doesn't like fish. Malcolm smiles calmly, trying to send the message that she needs to just shut up and deal. He switches plates with her as inconspicuously as possible.

But he can't eat that fish.

He's allergic to salmon.

I'm not even sure he can eat the potatoes or vegetables on the plate because they may have touched the salmon. Surely, she knows this. They've dated since puberty.

She's not actually going to let him eat that, is she?

I mean, holy shit, the guy shoved me into the pool and probably ruined my dress, but even I don't want him to have an allergic reaction.

"Hey, Mal," I say as casually as possible. "I was actually supposed to have the fish. I'll trade you plates if you'd rather have the prime rib."

The gratitude in his eyes is unmistakable. I forgot how soft his brown eyes can get when he's not acting like a clown, how kind he can be. He wasn't always a jerk. Sometimes he was nice when Brody wasn't. Sometimes, I wished he were my brother instead.

But right now, as he mouths *thank you* and passes his plate down to me, our eyes lock and heat floods my core.

It's only a moment. I tell myself it's just the dark hair and beard. The most basic attributes of my type. Clearly, my body has a reaction to that combo no matter whose face is underneath.

Weird. But bodies and brains do what they do, right?

Has he always had such a full bottom lip?

He's not having an allergic reaction already, is he?

He smiles when my plate reaches him. His plate reaches me at the same time, and I smile, too. I'm definitely having a reaction.

But this is not an allergy. And if there is a man in this world who I should be allergic to, it's Malcolm Fox.

Maybe it's a concussion. Come to think of it, I do feel a little dizzy. That has to be it. I obviously hit my head on the pool.

My brother extends his glass across the table and makes a comment that I can't hear. Malcolm lifts his in response. Damn, did he always have such big hands?

Oh, yeah. I am hopelessly concussed.

Over Dessert
Malcolm

Is IT NOT ENOUGH that Ellis looks just as sexy in the dress she's changed into than the black one she was wearing before? Okay, green, whatever. But does she still have to have such a soft heart, too?

She remembers that I'm allergic to salmon. She should hate me right now, and maybe she does, but at least she doesn't want me to risk anaphylactic shock.

My date, on the other hand? Celeste is just happy she got the meal she wanted.

I don't like her.

I've known for years that I don't love Celeste, but I didn't realize until just now that I don't even like her. If we just met for the first time, I wouldn't entertain the thought of dating her. We keep drifting back together, but we can't make it last for more than a few weeks. We're not compatible at all, anymore, not in any way. Maybe we never were.

We're not even really seeing each other right now. I just needed a date, and she was the familiar option.

We're too old for this shit. It needs to end. For good.

I don't want her to come to the wedding tomorrow. The thought of having to cater to her and listen to her whine about every little thing throughout the reception makes me want to crawl out of my skin.

Celeste can't stand not being the center of attention. She's the worst possible option for a wedding date. We've been to so many weddings together. I know how she behaves at them. Why did I think she was a good choice for my best friend's?

This is one wedding I actually want to be at, and she's going to ruin it for me.

No way am I going to let that happen. We just have to get through dinner.

Not seeing me anymore isn't going to break her heart. I know she doesn't love me either. Maybe she doesn't even like me anymore. We might finally have something in common.

But she really doesn't deal well with rejection. I'm going to have to handle this delicately.

When the dessert comes out, I'm served the chocolate cake instead of the cheesecake. At least I'm not allergic to chocolate.

Thankfully, Celeste gets her cheesecake, so she has nothing to complain about.

I can't help but glance over at Ellis' dessert plate. She has cheesecake. Maybe it's what she wants, but I can't imagine her not choosing chocolate cake. It was always her favorite. Anything chocolate was her favorite.

She catches me looking and gives a small shrug. It's not a shrug of confusion. That shrug says, *Oh, well. Guess I'll deal with it.* Her eyes go to my plate, and then she glares at me. But it's a teasing glare. I know the difference. Ellis French has a full spectrum of glares, and I've been on the receiving end of all of them through the years.

I point at my plate and mouth, *Do you want to trade?*

Her eyes light up and her head bobs up and down excitedly. I don't know how she can be so damn sexy and adorable at the same time.

Honestly, I always thought she was cute, but the sexiness is new. So new that I'm still questioning how that woman can possibly be Brody's sister. But when she smiles and her face lights up at the prospect of chocolate cake, she's undoubtedly Ellis.

Passing my plate down to her, I can't stop staring. I know the girl who always chooses the chocolate cake, but I'd give anything to get to know the woman who chooses dresses that make me want to forget whose sister she is.

How long has it been since I've seen her? I think she was barely a teenager the last time we saw each other, but that can't be right.

Celeste eyes my slice of cheesecake as I lower the plate to the table in front of me. "Hey, switch with me. That one has more raspberry sauce."

"No."

"What did you just say to me?"

"I said no. Eat the one you were given."

"Fine. I'll be going straight home after this. You can spend the rest of the night with your hand and your fantasies. The real me will be out of reach." She stabs a raspberry with her fork and drags her teeth across the tines as she pulls it out of her mouth. "Far, far out of reach."

I may indeed be spending some time with my hand and my fantasies later, but Celeste won't be the woman starring in them. She will be far, far from my mind.

Definitely the Champagne
Ellis

MAREN, MY BEST FRIEND, was supposed to be my plus-one
for Brody's wedding. We've been each other's wedding dates
since we vowed two years ago to stop taking guys to weddings.
Receptions are so much more fun with each other than a date.
But she's in San Francisco on a work trip, so I'm flying solo at
my brother's reception.

Did I mention all my other friends are already married? Re-
gardless of what the internet would like us to believe, the con-
cept of marrying young is still alive and well.

Unfortunately, none of my young wedded friends have been
married long enough yet to be divorced, so Maren is still my only
viable plus-one.

I don't think I'm cynical about marriage in general, but I've
never been much of a team player, so it's probably not in the
cards for me. It's not that I can't get along with other people. I
just don't want their input or assistance on anything.

Happily single is a thing. It's my thing.

Brody and Amanda will be fine, though. I know my brother.
He can be a stubborn ass, but he's also loyal to a fault. And he
adores Amanda. She is pretty great, so I have to give him points

for choosing a good sister-in-law for me. Their wedding was beautiful and their marriage will be, too.

My happiness for them doesn't negate the fact that I'd rather be somewhere else right now, like at home on my couch in comfy clothes, watching trash TV and eating frozen waffles topped with whipped cream and the good maraschino cherries. Those cherries are my weakness.

I mostly stick to a tight budget so I can afford my mermaid needs, but I splurge on my favorite cherries. Just seeing the bright yellow and red label makes me happy.

"Please share whatever you're thinking about that put that big smile on your face." Malcolm slides into the empty chair next to me.

It was nice of him to give me his chocolate cake last night at the rehearsal dinner, but it didn't make up for knocking me into the pool, forcing me to get naked in the parking lot where his jealous girlfriend spotlighted us. Speaking of Celeste . . .

"Where is your girlfriend?"

"She hasn't been my girlfriend since college. Last night was a date of convenience."

"Couldn't find one of those for the wedding?"

"Not on such short notice, no. Where's your date?"

"I don't bring dates to weddings."

"Ah, you're that girl."

"What girl?"

"The one who comes single so she can hook-up with a groomsman."

"All the groomsmen are my brother's closest friends, so no, that was not my plan. And I don't do that at other weddings either. Is that what you're doing? Hoping to hook-up with a bridesmaid?"

"There is a distinct possibility I may be hoping for that. Aren't you supposed to be sitting with your family?"

"I started out sitting at the family table, but I went to the bathroom, and when I came back, this empty table looked more inviting."

"Is it okay if I share it with you?"

"Looks like you already are. There is a seat for you at the family table as well."

"You didn't answer my question."

"Oh, for fuck's sake. Yes, Malcolm, you can sit here." Why do his shoulders look so broad in that suit? Isn't black supposed to be slimming?

"Not that one. What were you thinking about before I interrupted?"

"Cherries."

"You must really like cherries."

"Maraschino cherries, but not the cheap ones. The best ones. Everybody wants to tour wineries and cheese factories in Italy. I want to tour the Luxardo distillery."

"Amarena cherries are actually better."

"Pfft. Doubt it."

"Trust me. The Luxardo distillery tour is cool though."

"You've been?"

"I have. For the record, some people want to tour olive oil factories while they're in Italy as well."

"Of all the obscure things you could nerd out over, how the hell did you pick olive oil?"

"You don't like olive oil?"

"I like it, but I don't want to make a career out of it."

"I did a study abroad summer in Italy."

"You toured an olive oil factory, fell in love, and the rest is history?"

"Pretty much."

"Why not cherries? You said you toured the Luxardo distillery, too."

"It's not the same. We toured olive groves and the local mill, and then we got to taste the oil and learn about recent changes to the cultivation and processing methods. It was such an old and vital industry, but still evolving. I went back on my own to ask questions I hadn't thought of during the tour. Some of the olive trees were over a hundred years old, some two hundred. The agricultural aspect of it was fascinating, but the history . . . there was just this romance to it all."

"You find olives romantic?"

"I think you probably have to experience it to understand."

"I'm positive I'd be more infatuated with the cherries."

"Well, you always were strange."

"Ha! Me? You were the strange one."

He laughs and nods. "I know. So, why do you want to be a professional mermaid?"

"Okay, first of all, I already am a professional mermaid. I'm just not a member of a siren pod. Yet. But I'm pretty sure I'm going to land an audition with the Fantasia Faeries soon."

"And they're a big deal, I take it?"

"Yes. If I get hired by them, I won't have to hustle freelance gigs anymore. It's sort of like the difference between juggling as a party performer and being a member of Cirque du Soleil."

"Huh. So, the fantasy fairies put on shows and people buy tickets?"

"Fantasia, not fantasy, but yes, they go on tour, and they get booked for aquarium shows and private events, too."

"Wild. I never knew."

"Well, I never knew people found olives erotic."

"I said romantic. There is a difference."

"The two can coexist."

"For the lucky ones."

Oof. My core should not be tingling because he said that. All he did was rightly state a simple fact. It is a lucky thing when romance and eroticism coexist. But for some reason, I respond by squirming in my seat. And that's just the reaction he can see. What is wrong with me?

Malcolm has always had that tilted smile, but something about his face overall has changed, almost giving his quirked mouth a hint of sex appeal. It no longer looks like the crooked grin of a goofball teenage boy who's trying too hard. There's a certain self-assuredness to it now.

But I don't even like cocky guys.

Maybe it's the way his eyes narrowed and glimmered when he said it. I do like when guys flirt with their eyes.

But regular guys, not Malcolm.

Maybe I'm shifting and sizzling because it's been such a long time since I experienced the lucky combination and it's made me particularly vulnerable to a deep voice and snake eyes.

Or maybe it's just the champagne making my brain fizzy. I think this is my third glass? It's definitely the champagne.

The string quartet that Brody and Amanda hired to provide background music during dinner is still playing, but the deejay has arrived and started to set up. That means it's finally time for the bride and groom to cut the cakes. Thank Neptune.

Confession time: Neptune may be the genesis of my attraction to bearded men. Something about the way he grips that trident. Big hands. Piercing eyes. Like I said, I have a type. I can't remember how old I was the first time I saw an image of him, but I distinctly remember how looking at him made me feel.

Hey, it starts somewhere for all of us, right?

Anyway, I'm sneaking out after the dessert plates have been picked up. Everyone should have enough alcohol on board by then not to notice my absence. I've smiled for pictures, made a toast to the happy couple, and hugged every distant relative who's recognized me.

My mother will probably notice I'm missing when the time comes to toss birdseed at my brother's face as he runs for a waiting car, pulling his beautiful bride behind him. But as tempting as that sounds, I'm peopled out.

Malcolm stands and holds a hand out to me. "What is that for?" I ask.

"We need to gather around Brody and Amanda to watch them cut the cake."

"There are plenty of people here to suffocate them during that ritual."

"But the best man and the groom's sister should not be missing from pictures as it happens."

"Are you on my mother's payroll?"

"No one is paying me. Believe it or not, I simply understand the social etiquette of the situation."

"Wow. I guess you learned about more than olives while you were in Italy."

"You guess correctly. But I've learned a thing or two since then as well."

His eyes do that thing again. And then his hand closes around mine, and he pulls me to my feet. My knees try to surrender as soon as I stand. He places his free hand on my hip to steady me. "Whoa, easy."

"I'm fine," I quip in a voice far too defensive.

"Yeah, you probably just stood up too fast." His voice isn't mocking. It's reassuring. Gentle. So deep. And the heat from his palm radiates through my dress, which doesn't help my sea legs at all.

"I haven't eaten much today. Maybe my blood sugar is low. Cake is probably a good idea."

"Cake is always a good idea."

I smile back at him and let him lead me to the circle that's forming around the table holding the elaborate wedding cake and the simple groom's cake covered in whipped chocolate ganache. Brody and I are as different as can be about most things, but our love of chocolate is as much a familial trait as our dusty green eyes.

We smile as we watch Amanda dodge Brody's attempt to smash cake in her face. She gets a direct hit on him, and we all laugh, even though it's obvious his attempt to block her was just for show. He was always going to let her smear buttercream across his mouth. My brother would do just about anything to make her happy.

Sometimes he's so uptight I worry about him, but then I remember he has Amanda, and I know he'll lighten up as soon as he sees her again.

"She's good for him," I say.

Malcolm nods. "Since the day they met. I assume you want chocolate?"

"Of course. What kind of person eats vanilla cake?"

"It's not plain vanilla. It has fruit filling."

"That is such a weird thing for you to know."

"I went with them to taste samples."

"Why?"

"They said I'm a food guy and they wanted my input."

"You actually went with them to their cake tastings?"

"I'm a good friend."

"Is there olive oil in the cakes?"

"Let it go, Bubbles."

Oh, no he did not drag out that old nickname he used to taunt me with! I slam a stiletto heel into his toes. "Listen, if I was any of the Power Puff Girls, I was Buttercup."

He winces and hops on his uninjured foot. "I didn't call you that because of the Power Puff Girls. It was because you were always practicing holding your breath in the pool."

"Ohhhhh. Damn, I always thought it was a Power Puff Girls thing."

"No, you stomping psycho. But Bubbles fits since you grew up to be a mermaid."

"Well, I still don't like it." I give his chest a hard poke with my finger, and then point it back at myself. "And I'm still Buttercup if we're talking Power Puff Girls."

"Noted."

"But also, don't call me Buttercup."

"You got it, princess."

I glare at him. He takes a step back.

Nobody's Business
Malcolm

I SHOULD STOP WATCHING Ellis savor her chocolate cake, mainly because she does it in a way that if she livestreamed it, would earn her more money than those fantasy fairies ever could. If she ate chocolate cake like this while wearing her mermaid costume? Sweet Jesus.

What kind of wood is this flooring made from? Maybe it's oak. Could be maple. Probably not pine.

"Ouch." I rub my arm where Ellis has pinched it. "Why do you keep abusing me?"

"Have you been listening to me?"

"Yes."

"Then what did I just ask you?"

"You asked me something?"

She sighs. "I asked if you'd get me another glass of champagne. My mother is watching me like a hawk. She met me at the bar on my last trip and informed me I needed to slow down."

"Do you feel like you need to slow down?"

"No. I feel fine, except for the fact that I'm out of champagne and this cake is dry. It needs champagne."

"Would water possibly work?"

"No, it would not. Is your cake not dry?"

"Nope. The fruit filling keeps it moist."

"I hate that word."

Her cringe is pretty damn cute, but I'm smart enough not to tell her I think so.

"What word, moist? Seems like an inconvenient word for a mermaid to hate. I mean, you're probably moist more often than—" My words stop abruptly, as if I just took an ax to the vocal cords. Fuck. I didn't mean that to sound dirty, but now that it's out of my mouth, I'm pretty sure it did.

"Stop saying that word! More often than what?"

"I just meant that you spend a lot of time in water, so obviously . . . I'm going to go get you another glass of champagne now."

"Thanks."

I return with two flutes of champagne to find her closing her glossy coral lips around a forkful of my boring vanilla cake.

She pulls the fork from her mouth and smiles up at me as she eats the generous bite. "You're right. This one isn't dry."

Setting the glasses on the table, I smile back at her.

She eyes me suspiciously. "You have no smartass remark about me stealing a bite of your cake?"

"None at all."

"Why not? Did you hit your head on the way back from the bar?"

"Has anyone ever told you that you have an incredibly seductive mouth?"

She quickly covers her lips with her napkin, pretending to wipe at the corners, but I've caught her off-guard. And I like knowing I've unlocked some bashful recess of her personality. I like it entirely too damn much.

Ellis lays the napkin across her lap again, and straightens her shoulders as if I hadn't had her on the brink of blushing just seconds ago. "I assume you don't mean the way I talk."

"Your sarcasm is not at all what I meant."

"Aw, my sweet talk doesn't do it for you, huh?"

It's cute the way she's trying to match my confidence right now, but there's still a twinge of uneasiness in her tone. The biting edge her voice normally carries has softened. She really does sound a little sweet.

I know it's risky to let this part of me keep rising to the surface, but I do absolutely nothing to tamp it down. I want to play. And not role-play as the guy she used to know, the one who argued with her and teased her like a second big brother.

No, I want to play as the grown man I am now, a man who enjoys wicked flirtations that lead to hot, raw sex. The kind my instincts tell me she enjoys as well. Even as I'm having these thoughts, I know it's highly likely I'm going to regret it if I take a chance and tease her the way I want. If she shuts me down, I'll spend the rest of the night with my tail between my legs.

But if she doesn't . . . if that fire in her eyes reignites . . . if she wants to play, too . . . this night could change both our lives.

For better or for worse.

"Your pretty little mouth doesn't need to say anything at all to do it for me."

Did she just quiver in her chair? So, I've possibly got a shot here?

She downs half a flute of champagne, places the glass delicately back onto the table, and traces the tip of her tongue around the inner edges of her lips while her glassy eyes survey me. She's weighing the risks now, too.

The deejay announces it's time for the bride and groom to make their way to the floor for their first dance as husband and wife. Everyone around us claps, but we sit with our eyes locked on each other. We sip our champagne, never breaking our stares. Trying to read each other's thoughts.

I'm distantly aware of a song ending and another one beginning and bodies moving in the background, but Ellis French is too captivating for me to focus on anything other than her contemplative eyes.

What's it gonna be, beautiful?

"Let's dance." All hesitation is gone from her tone now, but she's not deflecting by suggesting we dance. She's attempting to gain some control of the situation.

Her voice is brazen but tempered. I think Ellis French might put up a bit of a fight after all, but not in the way I'd originally feared. I think this brat plans on fighting to keep her true nature under wraps.

But letting her hide from me is not in my nature. I want the real her, and I'm pretty sure I know how to coax her out to play.

Gary French watches me over his wife's shoulder as I lead his daughter onto the dance floor. He gives me a curt nod and a half-smile. His skeptical expression makes it clear he's wary of my intentions. But he shouldn't be.

Because my intentions with his grown daughter are none of his business. Not his or anyone else's.

One More Dance

Ellis

I FORGOT MALCOLM CAN actually dance. It's not like I've ever danced with him before, but I watched him and Brody dance with girls, wondering if boys would want to dance with me like that someday.

The man holding me against his chest right now wouldn't have given me the time of day back when he was practically living at our house, let alone given me a dance. Not that I'd have wanted to dance with him back then. But the way he's spinning me around tonight feels like we've done it a thousand times before.

My head keeps spinning after he pulls me back into him. Whoops. Who decided a disco ball would be a good idea? The tiny mirrored squares cast bouncing lights across the floor. The ball spins and the bouncing lights ride on waves. Is the floor rippling?

"I need to sit down."

"You're okay." Malcolm's deep voice sounds a lot more certain than I feel. "I've got you."

His body is so solid and warm. He turns me, and with a hand on my lower back, he guides me off the dance floor. He does such a good job keeping me moving in a straight line I think there is a chance no one else even realizes I'm dizzy.

"Are you going to be sick?" he asks as he pulls his chair closer to mine, keeping his voice low enough only I can hear.

"No. I don't feel sick. Just got dizzy all of a sudden. My stomach churned a little when it first happened, but I'm good now."

"Water?"

"Air would be better."

"Yeah, it's hot in here. Come on." He takes my hand and helps me to my feet.

My other hand drags my purse off the table and takes it with us.

A burst of cool night air sweeps over my shoulders as soon as we step outside. It's late April, and the days are already getting hot, but the temperature still gets a little chilly once the sun goes down. It's still layer weather, but I didn't bring a jacket, not even a wrap. My dress suddenly feels too summery.

Like he can read my mind, Malcolm whips off his jacket and drapes it over my shoulders. Warmed by his body heat, the satin lining provides a hug that melts my goosebumps immediately.

We walk down the sidewalk away from the building. "Thanks for getting me out of there without a scene."

"No worries. We can stay out here as long as you want."

"I think I'm going to head home, actually."

"You mean, as in drive yourself home?"

"Yeah."

"No way. I'll drive you."

"But my car—"

"Will be perfectly safe here."

I don't argue, partly because I know he's right, and partly because I want to see what he has in mind. Is he going to drive me straight home or does Malcolm have moves off the dance floor, too? It's not a thought I should even consider, but my body feels snug and warm in his jacket. "I want to dance some more. My hips are loose. They're not ready to stop moving."

"You want to go back inside?"

"No. I want to go somewhere else."

"Where did you and your loose hips have in mind?"

I shrug, and his jacket slips off my shoulders. He catches it and pulls it back up for me.

"Good reflexes for an olive oil broker." I stumble over a crack in the sidewalk.

Malcolm steadies me. "You're not very graceful for a mermaid."

"It's easier to be graceful in the water. Let's go to my parents' house and swim."

"No. That's a terrible idea."

"Why? They'll be here all night. It's been nearly twenty-four hours since you and I were in a pool together."

"You have had too much alcohol to get in a pool."

"Okay, grandpa." My heel catches on another crack in the concrete. "This place is in complete disrepair. What a disgrace. I remember when this club used to be nice."

Malcolm's hands are firm on my arms as he guides me back onto the sidewalk. "You always hated this place."

"I liked the pool. And the desserts."

"Right. Back before the chocolate cake got so dry."

"Yeah! Even the food has gone downhill."

He laughs, and I wonder what I said that was funny. I mostly want to know so I can say it again because his laugh tickles the little hairs on the back of my neck.

"You're going to take me straight home, aren't you?"

"It was not my original plan, but I think it's probably for the best tonight."

"Because you think I've had too much to drink."

"I'm not here to judge how much is too much, but I think you've had too much for us to go anywhere else and drink more. And I know you've had too much for me to take you to my place."

"You were thinking you might take me to your place?"

He looks at the ground, but I can see the corner of his sly smile. "Guilty."

"And you just assumed I'd say yes to that?"

"I never assume anything. But there was a moment where I kind of liked my odds." He holds his car door open for me.

The leather of his passenger seat is cold on the backs on my legs through my dress. I tug his jacket tighter around me before I pull the seat belt across my body.

Lights whizz by on the freeway, becoming a single streak as I stare drowsily out the window. My eyelids are heavy, but I shake my head to stay awake. "You drive too fast."

"Do you feel sick?"

"Why do you keep asking me that? Are you used to women getting sick when they're around you?"

He laughs again. But what I said wasn't funny. It was mean, and I only said it because I'm upset that he thinks I'm too tipsy for him to shoot his shot. Despite the cards that life dealt him as a kid, he grew up to be a decent man. With a deep voice and a dark beard and big strong hands . . .

"Hey, Malcolm."

"Yes, Buttercup?"

Now I laugh because that was fair. "That moment where you liked your odds?"

"Yeah?"

"They were pretty good."

"I really wish you hadn't told me that."

"You know the effects of alcohol wear off, right? In an hour or so, I'll probably be totally sober."

His crooked grin is on full display now, and it tells me he likes the way I think. His eyes shimmer when he looks at me and says, "Where do you live?"

"Oh, yeah. You don't know my address. I guess you'll just have to take me to your place after all."

"Wouldn't you rather go to your place where you'll have your own toothbrush and your own bed?"

"Will you come inside and stay for a while?"

"For a little while."

When I smile, he adds, "Just long enough to make sure you're okay."

"You mean long enough to dance."

"We'll see."

"Well, I'm dancing with or without you."

Being in a moving car may heighten the effects of the glasses of champagne that I lost count of, but I can still dance. Either with him or for him. We'll see.

Time Flies
Malcolm

I WISH I'D NOTICED how much champagne Ellis drank throughout the night. Not that I could've stopped her from having another glass whenever she wanted simply by telling her no, but maybe I could've redirected her attention for a while in between glasses to space them out.

But I was too busy being mesmerized by her eyes and her smile and her body that I undeniably want to see more of. She thinks she's completely fine and knows what she's doing, and maybe she's right, but all I can think about is what happens if she's wrong.

Her potential for regret in the morning over any actions she may tipsily consent to tonight have thrown ice water on my dick. I may have let my impulse control get out of hand last night when I tackled her into the pool, but this is different.

With a woman I share no history with, there's no foundation to worry about damaging. If we wake up and decide we don't want to see each other again? Cool. We go on with our lives. No harm done.

Of course, it's not like Ellis and I regularly run into each other these days. We're practically strangers at this point. Hell, it had been so long since I last saw her that I didn't even recognize her. In the dark with her back to me, but still. Could it really have been as long as I think?

"When was the last time you and I saw each other before last night?"

"Um . . ." She twirls a section of her hair and chews on her bottom lip. "Probably Brody's graduation dinner. When he got his degree, not high school. We definitely saw each other a few times while y'all were in college because you'd come home with him for weekends and wipe out all my good snacks."

"Damn. That was almost eight years ago."

"Yep. I'd just turned sixteen. Got in a huge fight with my parents because they wouldn't let me take my best friend with us to Austin for the graduation, so I was pissed the whole time. I probably didn't say two words to anyone."

"They must not have liked your friend because they never said no when Brody asked if I could come with him somewhere. Hell, I tagged along for nearly all y'all's family events."

"I wanted to take my own car instead of riding with them."

"Ah, now I see the problem."

She rolls her eyes that I'm siding with her parents' logic, but she smiles right after. "It makes sense we hadn't seen each other in so long, though. Didn't you move away for a while?"

"Yeah, I moved to New York right after graduation. Did the Wall Street thing for a few years."

"I know. I was trying to be nice and not mention it."

"What does that mean?"

She bites down on her lip like she's still trying to avoid saying something.

"Why would I not want you to mention that I worked on Wall Street?"

"Because you got fired?"

"No, I didn't. What made you think that?"

"The first time we met Amanda was when Brody brought her to our mom's birthday dinner. While we were eating, Dad asked about you, and Brody said that you weren't working on Wall Street anymore. He said you wanted a change, so you were going back to school. In the car on the way home, Dad said he knew Brody was lying. You know how his nostrils flare when he lies? Anyway, Dad said no one who'd been lucky enough to land a job like the one you had would quit at your age, so he was sure you'd been fired, but Brody just didn't want to say it in front of his girlfriend."

"Brody wasn't lying. If his nostrils flared, it was probably because I didn't go back to school in the traditional sense. I took a class to become an olive oil sommelier, a professional taster. After that, I interned with a producer in Spain, and then one in Italy. Spent some time in Portugal and South Africa to check out the industry in other countries. I can see why Brody didn't want to give all the details to your dad. He can be a harsh judge of things he doesn't understand."

"You don't say?"

"Oh, come on. Are you trying to tell me he's not crazy about his daughter being a professional mermaid?"

We share a laugh, commiseration over her father's scorn regarding our career choices.

Eight years is a long time. I see Brody regularly, and he talks about Ellis often enough that I know some things about her life, but I can't believe it's been so long since I've seen her. Time flies. Little sisters grow up.

And sometimes, a best man isn't as good a man as he should be.

"You still haven't told me where you live."

"Mesa Canyon Apartments on Voss. You know, where there is no mesa and no canyon."

"Got it. I know exactly where that is. But your description could be anywhere in Houston. No canyons or mesas in this city that I'm aware of."

"True. At least there's a bakery next door."

"Well, if you can't have a view of a mesa or a canyon, I guess a bakery is the next best thing."

"Yeah, and it probably smells better anyway."

"There's always a silver lining."

I cut the wheel to turn into the parking lot of her apartments, and pull into an open spot right in front of her building.

"You can't leave your car here. This is short-term parking. Fifteen-minute limit, and they take it seriously."

"Do you really think they'll tow my car?"

"Trust me, it won't be here when you wake up in the morning."

"You're right. It'll be at my place because I'm not staying here overnight."

"You plan on leaving in less than fifteen minutes?"

"Fine." I back out of the space and park farther away, which I still think is probably unnecessary, but it makes Ellis smile. And I really like her smile.

It's the kind of smile that could make a man lose track of time, might cause him to stay somewhere longer than he intended.

Maybe moving the car was a good idea.

Expiration Dates

Ellis

I BOLT UPRIGHT IN my bed. What was that sound? Did a bird hit the window?

A quick glance at the unslept-on side of my bed starts a replay of last night. Rubbing my eyes doesn't make them hurt any less, but the room is slightly less blurry when I reopen them. If only I could wipe away the humiliating memory of how I threw myself at Malcolm.

And the fact that he turned me down.

Did I really attempt to give him a lap dance?

Oh, for the love of baby starfish, please let this be a bad dream.

A car alarm goes off on the street below my window. It sets off my neighbor's neurotic beagle, Meatball, who will howl nonstop until his owner takes him for a walk so he can confirm the alarm isn't signifying the end of the world.

My neighbor's door slams, and Meatball's howling fades as they head for the stairs. This is too much mundane reality for a dream.

It's real. Last night happened.

Malcolm Fox turned me down.

And then, in what might've been my most desperate move ever, I asked him to stay with me, anyway. It's all coming back to me now. In my mind, it was going to play out with him sleeping in my bed, where he'd surely change his mind once my warm, vulnerable body was so close to his and the sweet scents of my perfume and shampoo comingled and emanated from the fibers of my sheets and the temptation to touch me would become overwhelming until he could no longer resist . . .

He declined that offer, too.

Another thump pulls my attention toward the hall outside my bedroom. That sound is coming from inside my apartment. Wait. He stayed? And he's still here?

I throw myself back down onto the mattress and pull a pillow over my face, but it's no use. I can hold my breath for three minutes. There's no way I'll be able to suffocate myself.

There is a third thump, and then a fourth right after it. What is he doing, playing wall ball in my living room?

It is him, right?

My feet shuffle down the hall toward the thumping noise while my leg muscles protest, begging me to lie back down. When I round the corner, my trashcan comes into view, sitting in the center of the kitchen with the lid resting on the floor next to it.

Malcolm takes a free throw shot with my olive oil, causing another thump.

"What the hell are you doing?" I rush the trashcan and rescue my olive oil. "This stuff is eight bucks!"

"Eight bucks." He shakes his head. "For olive oil in a plastic bottle. Not that anything leeching out of plastic is going to hurt that already toxic crap."

"Toxic?" I point to the label, running my fingertip under the words as I read. "It's extra virgin."

"No, it's not. It's not even olive oil."

"Oh, okay, genius. Then what is it?"

"Probably some sort of seed oil, maybe mixed with vegetable oil. Who knows? There might be a small amount of olive oil in there, but it's not pure olive oil, and it's damn sure not extra virgin olive oil."

"What are you, an expert?" *Oh, shit.*

"Yes! That is exactly what I am."

I peer into the trash to see what made the first few thump sounds. "Why are you throwing out all of my groceries?"

"I'm only throwing out the stuff that's expired."

"Do you do this at everyone's house?"

"I opened the fridge to get some water and saw your salad dressing collection. I was curious, so I started reading the labels. They were all expired, Ellis. Like so expired you could die if you eat them."

"Okay, nobody's dying. If I'd known the salad dressing police were coming, I'd have thrown them out myself. I haven't eaten any of those dressings since before they expired. Sometimes, I buy something new because it sounds interesting, but then I don't like it, so I don't eat it again."

"So, you just keep it in your fridge as a souvenir of your bad decision?"

"It stays in my fridge because I forget about it."

"How can you forget about it when it's right there every time you open the door?"

I shrug. "It no longer interests me, so I just don't see it anymore."

"That makes no sense."

"You know what makes no sense? Cleaning out a stranger's refrigerator."

"We're not strangers."

"That's your rebuttal?" I set my olive oil in its usual spot on the counter.

Malcolm grabs it and tosses it back into the trash.

I retrieve it again, but he defends my whole counter with his body—arms spread, moving side-to-side, blocking my attempt to put the plastic bottle back where it goes.

Raring back my arm, I prepare to leave a round indentation in his forehead. "So help me, Malcolm, if you don't move out of my way."

"I promise to replace it with real olive oil if you will please just throw that shit away."

"You'll give me the good stuff?"

"Very good stuff."

"Stuff that costs more than eight dollars a bottle?"

He pinches the bridge of his nose. "Yep. More than eight bucks a bottle."

I drop my olive oil into the trash. "Fine, but you better come through quick. I use a lot of olive oil."

"I'm pretty sure you've never used olive oil in your life."

"You're kind of a snob, do you know that?"

"Yes, I am an unapologetic olive oil snob."

"Why are you still here? Did you sleep in my bed?"

"Trust me, I didn't plan to be. And no, I slept on your couch. I planned to get a drink of water, check on you one last time, and then head out. But I got distracted."

"What do you mean check on me one last time? How many times did you check on me?"

"I checked to be sure you were okay before I turned the TV off last night. And I checked on you again when I woke up this morning."

"That's creepy."

"No, that's caring."

"Well, thank you for caring." I tug down the hem of my tank top, suddenly feeling self-conscious about standing in front of him in nothing but a tank and a thong. "But maybe do it in a less creepy way from now on."

"Will you please stop pulling down the top of your shirt?"

"I'm not pulling down the top of it. I'm pulling down the bottom."

"Yeah, well, doing one causes the other."

"You find my boobs distracting?"

"Yes."

"Huh. It's a shame you weren't so easily distracted last night."

"I was very easily distracted last night, but . . ."

"But what? Please, go on. I can't imagine anything you have to say at this point could make things any worse between us."

"You're Brody's sister. And I couldn't stand the thought that if we had sex, you might avoid me for the rest of your life."

"Holy shit. How bad are you at sex?"

"I'm quite good at it, but your inhibitions were lowered by alcohol, and I didn't want to take advantage of you."

"Nah, cat's out of the bag now. You suck at sex." I step close enough to poke him in the chest. "That's why you wouldn't go through with it."

He grabs my wrist to stop me from stabbing him with my finger again. His grip is firm. I use my other hand to poke him so he'll take that wrist, too. Call it an experiment. One that yields exactly the results I expected.

His hands hold my wrists captive, and his smoldering gaze does the same to my eyes. "I am not bad at sex, sweetheart, and there was a time I would've been eager to prove that to you, but I no longer do things for the sake of proving myself to anyone."

"Fine. Then think of it as me proving myself to you."

What the fuck am I saying? Am I drunker now than I was last night? Last night was the heat of the moment. I don't have an excuse for desperately coming on to him this morning.

"You cannot possibly think I doubt how good you'd be." He kisses my forehead, and then he releases my wrists.

And that's it. The moment's over.

"I guess I look like an idiot right now." I resist the urge to tug on my tank top again.

"Please don't feel that way." He runs his hand through his hair. "I didn't just naturally outgrow my issue with self-control, Ellis. I worked hard to overcome it. Sometimes good things have a downside. I'm not really a spontaneous guy these days. I can't act on impulse anymore. Sometimes, I think I can, but then the questions have to be answered. Is this a good idea? Will I regret it? Will it have a negative consequence?"

"You never have one-night-stands? No casual sex ever?"

His eyes cloud. "Not unless I've answered all the questions first."

"With a stranger, you can tell yourself it's a good idea and you won't regret it and there will be no negative consequences."

"Yeah, usually. But we're not strangers."

So, it's not just a no, it's a never. Got it.

"Don't forget you owe me olive oil."

"I'll bring it by later."

"I probably won't answer the door."

"I'll knock when I leave it on the mat, and then I'll walk away so you don't have to see me."

He kisses my forehead again before he steps past me and heads for my front door.

"Make it two."

"What?"

"Two bottles. Like I said, I use a lot of olive oil."

"I'll stock you up, Buttercup."

His grin disarms me. I'm not even mad at him for calling me Buttercup. "Hey, Malcolm."

"Yeah?"

"I wasn't dangerously drunk or anything. You didn't need to stay here and check on me throughout the night."

"I stayed because I was exhausted, didn't feel like driving home."

I don't believe he was too tired to drive. He's just saying that because he doesn't want to admit the real reason he stayed.

"Did you even once think about coming to my room and climbing into bed with me?"

"No." He opens my door to leave, but pauses before he steps out of my apartment. With his back to me, he says, "I thought about it a lot more than once."

The door shuts gently behind him.

A whimper escapes me, and I'm grateful he's on the other side of the door and can't hear it. When did I get this pathetically needy?

I know a few men who'd be more than willing to fulfill my needs right now. And they don't worry about the dates on anything in my fridge or what kind of oil I buy. They don't care about anything but having a good time in the moment. Malcolm cares too much about what might come after.

Neptune knows I wish he cared less—just enough less to fuck me without seeing me as a mistake.

At least I know he was tempted.

But if I'm a temptation he can resist, I'm not much of one at all.

Why is this happening now? I never even had a schoolgirl crush on him. Not for a minute. I cannot obsess over Malcolm Fox at this point in my life. The only obsession I can handle right now is training so I'll be ready when the Fantasia Faeries open auditions.

My sole focus needs to be on mermaiding. A little time in the pool will probably clear my head.

But I've recently promised management I won't use the pool downstairs for training in my tail. Apparently, it bothers some of my neighbors. People are bizarre.

My parents have a pool, but my dad swears the metallic paint and glitter from my tail is bad for the filter. It doesn't come off in the pool, but he can't be convinced he's wrong. Ever.

I wonder if Malcolm has a pool. Too bad I don't have his number to ask. I probably wouldn't anyway.

Mom might have his number. Not that I'm going to ask her for it. I'm one-hundred percent definitely not doing that. Never.

The gym. I need to go to the gym. I'll swim later. Here. Without my tail. It'll be fine.

In Case of Emergency
Malcolm

I KEPT MY WORD and didn't wait for Ellis to come to the door when I dropped off three bottles of better oil than she's ever had—just a quick knock and I walked away. I'm dying to reach out to make sure she brought them in. It's too warm outside for that oil to sit there all afternoon.

But I don't even have her number, which suddenly seems wrong. There could be a million reasons I might need to reach out to her regarding Brody. It could be an emergency.

Right. Like the many emergencies involving her brother that have happened over the past eight years.

Eight years gone and I haven't missed having her in my life. What an asshole. We were practically family.

I don't guess she's missed me either. Why do I miss her now? That's what this feeling is. I miss her. At a level I have no right to. No reason to. I want to take her to dinner and get caught up on eight-years-worth of her life, to hear about every moment I've missed.

This makes no damn sense. It's not like we shared some intense bond when we were growing up. She was just there.

Brody's little sister. An extension of my best friend. But now she's this . . . this full-grown woman!

An intriguing, funny, sexy, magnetically irresistible woman—one who I have to resist. Resisting her should be easy because one, she's Brody's sister, and two, I don't like complications in my life.

And Ellis French is complicated. She's not for me.

This is just a passing attraction that probably feels like a bigger deal than it actually is because of the shock of realizing it was her next to the pool the other night. That's all.

I'm nearly thirty and fully committed to eternal bachelorhood. I never get attached to new women. She's not new, though. Yet, in so many ways, she totally is.

I prop my elbows on my kitchen counter and hold my forehead while I contemplate the veins in the granite. Anything to stop thinking about her. My mind is so fucked right now.

The microwave dings, and I pull out the leftover Mediterranean chicken and lentils that I've reheated. At three days old, it might be questionable, but it came from a good restaurant. Besides, I'm dousing it in extra virgin olive oil.

Little known fact: it's antifungal and antibacterial.

Lesser known fact: I might occasionally trust the effectiveness of those properties more than I should.

On the other hand, I haven't had food poisoning since college, so who's to say?

I ignored two invitations to meet friends for dinner tonight, telling myself I didn't want to waste these leftovers. It's true I hate to waste food, but I also knew all I'd want to talk about is Ellis. It's bad enough I'm making things weird in my own head.

Celeste has shown up in my social media feeds repeatedly today, all with quotes about the joys of being a strong, independent woman and how change is necessary for growth. She's always preferred to process things in a public way.

I feel nothing when her face pops up on my phone. No hard feelings or bitterness. Hell, I'm as guilty as she is for prolonging our inevitable end. But I don't feel any fondness either. All I feel is lighter, free in a way I didn't realize I wasn't before.

And horny. God, am I horny. Not in a way that makes me want to reach out to an ex either. I want to reach out to someone who is sort of new. It's probably a good thing I don't have Ellis's number.

What I do have is her most recent profile picture staring back at me from my phone screen. Her eyes are bright and her full lips are shiny. She's lying on a rock ledge overlooking a waterfall spilling into a pool. That shimmery bikini top is hard to look away from. Her entire lower half is hidden in a glittery green tail, but the curves of her waist and hips make me want to grip them and pull her against me.

She looks so happy. Her mermaid name is Ellisandra, which makes me laugh because it's just so her. It sounds like something she and her best friend would've come up with when they were in middle school.

It's not that I think it's childish. I get that it's important to her, but having an alternate mermaid persona is a world I don't know anything about. My curiosity is piqued, though, and when that happens, I usually have to dig in until I at least understand the premise.

All I know right now is that the sexiness of her alternate persona is unsettling. I've never had mermaid fantasies.

Not before this picture, anyway.

And That's a Wrap
Ellis

WHAT A FREAKING WEEK. I've been working ridiculous hours as a makeup artist for a movie that's shooting entirely in abandoned buildings spread from Galveston to Conroe.

I'll never understand why these scenes couldn't all be filmed in one place. By the time they're done getting the buildings ready to film in, they look basically the same, anyway.

I'm grateful for the job, and I usually love doing special effects makeup, but everything about this film is bizarre from the script to the set locations. There's a fine line between going the extra mile for authenticity and doing it just because you can.

I'd like five minutes alone with the first reporter who referred to this producer as an eccentric filmmaking savant. He created a monster.

I'm exhausted. It's been five days of sitting in hours of traffic to do constant touch-ups on uncomfortable, irritable actors amidst unceasing yelling from the director who demanded retake after retake after retake.

Thank goodness I'm coming in at the end after everyone's already been exposed to the radiation. No one has long to live at this point. Soon I'll be free to return to what matters most in my life.

My salad greens are past their prime, but they're still usable. I shake on more feta cheese and sprinkle some pumpkin seeds on top. Out of sheer stubbornness, I've avoided trying Malcolm's fancy olive oil, but since he threw mine out and the contents in this bowl are basically all I have left in my apartment to eat, the moment of truth has come.

I give it a sniff before I drizzle it onto my salad. Peppery and green. But, also almost a little nutty? It doesn't smell like any olive oil I've ever smelled before. Logically, I know that confirms Malcolm's claims that I've never had good EVOO, but I'm still resentful of this stuff. I squeeze a lemon over the bowl and toss.

This is a pretty good salad. Not as good as pizza, but I'm determined to cut down on food delivery expenses. And internet impulse buys.

Mermaid life ain't cheap.

As I bring the fork closer to my face, I notice my cuticle situation. It's not good. I mentally add a manicure to my weekend errands list. One of these days I'll start making regular appointments.

Maren texts to confirm that I haven't forgotten about brunch on Sunday. If I had put that event on my actual calendar in my phone instead of just the one in my head, I'd be able to tell her truthfully that I hadn't forgotten.

> *I wouldn't miss brunch with your family for anything. Except an audition with the Fantasia Faeries, but you already knew that.*

The women in her family do a monthly brunch, and there are a lot of women in Maren's family. If everyone was able to show up for the same brunch, they'd probably have to rent out a hotel ballroom. Sometimes they meet at someone's house, and sometimes it's at a restaurant, assuming they reserve the space far enough ahead of time. The guest list is long, even when several of them can't make it.

Invites are open to everyone from her teen cousins to her grandmother, and it's always a good time—especially when Maren's mom is the host.

Her mom is a cross between Martha Stewart and Beth Dutton from *Yellowstone*. Her name is actually Beth, too. Her Martha side hosts brunch in her house, where she serves mimosas in vintage crystal stemware, makes all the elaborate seasonal table centerpieces herself, and won't let anyone leave without a gift bag, but if you crossed her or her family, I wholeheartedly believe Dark Beth would surface, and she wouldn't hesitate to feed you to the hogs.

They don't own hogs, but she's also the kind of woman who can source what she needs in the most unlikely of situations. I once watched her summon a limo at nine pm in a small beach town on the Oregon coast with a single phone call. She did not do a search for a limo company, nor did she sound like she was speaking to a dispatcher from any kind of car service. She simply gave the address to whomever answered her call and said, "There are six of us. We want champagne on the way there and we will need snacks on the way home."

Where were we going? To Portland for a midnight concert, which we found out about due to a single phone call she'd received five minutes earlier. We were there for a four-day girls' trip, and she hooked up tickets to an unannounced show and a limo to get us there like we were celebrities. The woman has mysterious connections.

Maybe they're sketchy. Who knows? They arrive with bubbles and charcuterie, though, so how dangerous could they be?

I love Maren's entire family. And my family adores her.

During the summer after we graduated from high school, Brody seemed to like her a little too much. She'd just turned eighteen, and he was nearly twenty-four. She wasn't technically a minor, anymore, but it was still uncomfortable as hell for me. He insisted he wasn't trying to flirt with her until I almost believed him.

But he definitely didn't shun the attention when she flirted with him. I basically told Maren if she made that mistake, I never wanted to know about it. She agreed that was probably for the best. I never told Brody anything other than I would destroy him if he dared.

To this day, they both insist he never dared, although when it's just me and her, Maren readily admits she'd have been more than willing if he'd made the slightest move back then because she was borderline obsessed with him—as if I didn't know. She outgrew her fascination with him, thankfully.

I can still get angry thinking about the way Brody flirted with her (because yes, he did!) and how she flirted back like they weren't practically related.

Brody would have the same reaction right now if he knew about the feelings I'm fighting when it comes to his best friend. It's not at all the same thing, though. I'm the age now that Brody was back then, but his friend is a full-grown man who can't be tempted, not barely legal and infatuated.

We're only six years apart, but back then, six years felt like a bigger gap. The space between eighteen and twenty-four felt like an entire generation to me. Probably because I'd always looked at Brody as being so much older. But the space between twenty-four and nearly thirty feels like nothing at all.

Which is clearly what's going to happen between Malcolm and me: Nothing at all. Dammit.

> *Yay! Come early so I can tell you again all the reasons you should keep trying to seduce your brother's best friend. I've come up with a few new ones. And Mom has thoughts, too.*

Listening to the dynamic duo of Maren and her mom, Beth, scheming to get a certain bearded olive oil broker between my legs is not going to be a highlight of my weekend.

I'll endure it, but I'm going to ignore it until they have me backed into a kitchen corner and are plying me with mimosas and fancy cheese.

It won't shock me at all if her mom has a spiritual matchmaker on speed dial.

I sink down into my steaming bubble bath until my aching shoulders are submerged. Another exciting Friday night.

In the Name of Research
Malcolm

MY EYES BURN FROM staring at the computer all day. I promised myself weeks ago that I'd stop working on Saturdays, but every time I log on to do one quick thing, hours fly by before I realize I've worked all day again.

It's like that when you're starting something new, I remind myself.

Okay, the truth is I only worked for a few hours this morning. The rest of the day, I was looking into what it takes to be a professional mermaid. The pools of information are deep, and I couldn't keep from diving into another one and then another. My burning eyes are probably the only reason I've come up for air.

Professional mermaiding is niche, but not as much as I'd assumed.

And now, I'm having strange thoughts—thoughts like how maybe I could host my next marketing event in a bar with a tank. Maybe a launch event? And maybe Ellis might want to be one of the mermaid performers. Or the only one?

I'd never want her to think I was offering her a gig because I didn't think she could get her own, though. It's not like that.

I mostly just want to see her as Ellisandra, to wave at her through the glass and tell people I know her. *She's amazing isn't she? Yeah, she's always loved the water.*

I'd be genuinely proud of her. I know I would be. And I know what it's like to wish someone who cared about you had your back, that they were proud of you. I've never had it, but I want it for her.

These mermaids work so hard at a job that most people either don't know exists or they take for granted when they see a show. It's just people swimming around in a tail. No big deal.

But they're wrong. It is a big deal.

I've watched dozens of mermaids swim across my monitor today, but all I can think is how her moves are probably more fluid, her hair probably fans out prettier, her bubble kisses probably last longer . . .

I'm an idiot. No other man would've turned Ellis down the night of Brody's wedding. My fist clenches with the urge to punch these hypothetical other guys.

I should punch myself.

Fuuuuck.

Why can't I let this go? I know I did the right thing. Ellis and I can't happen, not even once. We haven't spoken since I left her apartment, but I can't get her out of my head. And I want her more every day.

I need some fresh air. And paper towels, which I could get delivered, but I need to get out of here before I click another mermaid related link.

Traffic streams past the exit to my parking garage. Not one driver will pause to let me out. I'm at the mercy of the traffic light at the intersection and the cars turning into my path off side streets.

Trying to pull out of here is always a nightmare on the weekends and in rush hour, which is why I opt to ride my skateboard to work most days. My office is just a few blocks away. It's a matter of convenience, but it's somehow made me just quirky enough to attract local media attention.

Don't get me wrong, I'm grateful for the interviews, but I wish they'd focus a little more on the products I'm bringing to the market instead of how I get to the office where it happens.

I could work entirely out of my condo, but it's too easy for me to stay home as it is. There was a time when I was never home, but lately, it's where I most want to be. I know getting out is healthier, but staying home makes me happier these days.

I'm not a recluse, but I don't enjoy the bar scene anymore. When you're living that life, it's hard to imagine the day will come when it doesn't hold anything for you. I always assumed people stopped going out every night because they got married and had kids.

I haven't done either of those things, and I don't see them happening in my life. Thirty is lurking. I know that's not old, but I never click with anyone new. And there's no ex who I want a second chance with.

If no one new clicks and no one old beckons, that leaves no one at all.

Just me and the mermaids.

My smile quickly turns to a wince at that thought. I really only want one mermaid.

A car slows to drop someone off on the sidewalk, and I gun it a little harder than necessary as I drive into the hole they've created in traffic.

Adjusting my speed, I shake my head to clear away the distracting thoughts. My only mission right now is to obtain paper towels and whatever other household items I've forgotten I put on my list.

I've been making a list that pertains to Ellis, too. Only in my head, but it's a growing list, weighing all the pros and cons, and totally ignoring the possibility that my chance is probably already gone.

The Call of the Ocean

Ellis

THIS WEEK HAS REQUIRED less time in traffic, but I've been on my feet longer every day, and it's going to stay that way until Friday. I'm at the midpoint, so at least the end is in sight, but the thought of two more ridiculously long days split between seeing clients in the spa and transforming actors on location is draining my life force.

I love my jobs. I love my jobs. I love my jobs.

Wine won't make it better. I don't want junk food or trash TV. This rarely happens, but I'm totally spent, nothing left to give. Too tired to eat. Being in bed this early feels a little sad, but not so much that I want to get back up.

The only thing that could possibly rejuvenate me is an email. I close my eyes and repeat my weekly affirmation: *My dreams are coming true every day.*

I open my eyes and then my inbox. There was a time I had no idea what emails I was ignoring, and I was perfectly happy. But back then, my shot at my dream job didn't hinge on an emailed invitation for an audition. I cleared out thousands of old messages to make sure the only one I care about won't get lost.

Even my spam folder gets cleared daily now.

Tonight, my inbox holds a notice from my gym, thanking me for my automated payment, which hits like a subliminal jab for not showing up regularly anymore. If I need refills for my aromatherapy atomizer, now is the time to order. Fifteen percent off. An online boutique I ordered a sweater from months ago misses me—not enough to try to woo me back with a discount, apparently. Delete.

Mom has sent a recipe she says I asked for, though I think she may have meant to send it to Amanda. That seems like something a good daughter-in-law might ask her for, right? It for sure doesn't ring any bells for this good daughter. I save it, anyway.

I check my spam folder, just to be sure. It's not there either.

The Fantasia Faeries haven't sent me anything. Not yet.

A quick check of their website confirms they haven't posted a notice about auditions there either.

It's still going to happen for me.

Their website is impressive. I wish I could send it anonymously to my parents to make them see this as a serious business. There are video clips from recent performances and even some from their last round of auditions. The application link is right up top, along with their stringent requirements.

Obviously, it's real, and I'm not the only person in the world aspiring to join this pod.

Even if I could wing it into my parents' inboxes anonymously, they'd be about as likely to open the website as I am to open Mom's recipe for Marry Me Marinara.

I'd be more likely to open one for Fuck Me Fettuccini—topped with Keeping it Casual Carbonara.

At least I'm not too tired to amuse myself. That's probably a good sign.

But speaking of sex and food . . . I wonder what Malcolm's website looks like. What's the name of his company? Why don't I know that? Why would I?

I type his name into the search bar, figuring either nothing will come up or there will be a million links for random dudes also named Malcolm Fox. To narrow the results, I add Houston and olive oil to my search phrase.

A whole lot of links show up, but the Malcolms aren't random. It's him after him after him. Whoa. I click on an interview out of curiosity.

He's always been funny. Now he's also poised. Charming where he used to be chaotic. And smart. His responses are all so intelligent. Interesting.

That's a really good picture of him, too.

Every interviewer brings up the skateboarding to work thing. These people act like he's saving the planet with his zero-emissions transportation while simultaneously rescuing us all from the depths of our olive oil ignorance.

Not to mention his informative newsletter. He has a newsletter. And people subscribe to it—even read it, apparently.

I click the link at the bottom of the interview that's currently open on my screen. It takes me to his website. So many pages. This is way more expansive than I expected. There are pictures of him with famous chefs. Photos taken in olive orchards and mills and restaurants all over the world.

He might be an icon in his industry.

In the food world overall even.

To me, he's always just been Malcolm, Mal, my brother's best friend, the guy who could annoy me worse than Brody sometimes, and then turn right around and make me feel more special than anyone else ever did. Just Malcolm. Always around. No big deal.

I just found out that to a whole lot of other people, he's become an absolute big damn deal. His company is called Fox Olivo Imports, not something catchy or cutesy. It's strictly business.

He's a whole grown-ass businessman with connections all over the world. Admired by other people who are also big damn deals.

And I really believed I had a shot with him? Me with my multiple part-time hustles and my big mermaid dreams.

I thought we were so similar in our offbeat endeavors, but we couldn't be more different. We are not on the same level at all.

Dear Neptune! He must think I'm a complete joke. His best friend's drunken little sister who he felt obligated to take care of. How did I not realize this before?

He cleaned out my fridge because he thought I wasn't competent enough to avoid accidentally poisoning myself!

Maybe I'll just walk into the ocean and hope for real mermaids to save me from the memory of grinding on his erection with my dress twisted around my hips and mascara smeared under my eyes.

My only saving grace is knowing he'll never tell anyone. It's our pathetic little secret. The saddest part of all is that I wouldn't have minded being his dirty little secret. Might've loved it, in fact. But having this kind of a secret with him?

Yeah, the ocean is calling . . .

Special Delivery
Malcolm

I'M FINALLY DOING IT—NOT working on a Saturday. I haven't gone into the office. Haven't opened my laptop or my phone to check messages or follow up on anything, not even while I was waiting for my car to be washed and detailed. Social media posts and random articles are all I'm allowing myself to see.

I resisted the pull to look at my inbox while sitting at a red light on my way to pick up my laundry.

Didn't even sneak a quick peek while standing in line at the grocery store.

I'm killing it.

How can it only be noon?

Honestly, it might be smarter to dive into my emails than what I'm about to do next.

But this oil is incredible. And I want her to taste it. She deserves to taste an olive oil this special. Anything to keep her from going back to the stuff she's been buying. Not that she'll be buying this one, but maybe it will cement her appreciation for real olive oil.

I'm not going to tell her how expensive this small bottle of oil is. That's not the point. I just want to share it with her, to introduce her to the variances and complexities in genuine extra virgin olive oil.

I second guess myself all the way up the stairs. All the way to her door. But once I'm standing there, I realize I can't just knock, set it down, and walk away. It's too hot out here for this oil to sit on her mermaid welcome mat for hours.

What if she's not home? What if she's in the shower and doesn't hear me knock?

There's no choice. I have to knock and wait for her to answer. I'll just hand off the bottle with a brief explanation and leave. Hopefully, she'll take it. And not throw it at me.

She doesn't answer after my first attempt. If she really is in the shower, she wouldn't have heard me though, and I already drove all the way over here. May as well wait a few minutes and try again.

I lean against the wall next to her door, holding my exquisite oil like a lovesick teenager about to ask his crush to the prom. This is sort of like an adult promposal in a way. I'm not asking her to go anywhere with me or hoping she'll be my girlfriend, but I am inviting her to experience and enjoy something, hoping she'll appreciate the effort that went into it, that she'll feel even just a little of my passion.

For olive oil.

Yeah, this is ridiculous. I should go.

"What are you doing here?"

Shit. Too late.

Ellis's voice comes from the top of the stairs. She wasn't in the shower. She was at the pool. That probably should've been one of my guesses.

"I knocked, but when you didn't answer I thought you might be in the shower."

Her hair hangs over her shoulders in damp waves. She's wearing a turquoise bikini top with a short floral wrap skirt tied at her waist and flip-flops with thin leather straps.

She looks like she should be in an ad for a cruise line or a tropical resort. Carefree. Effortlessly gorgeous.

As she walks closer, I notice the sun has made the tiny freckles on her cheeks brighter. Her lips are coated with something that makes them shiny, probably a lip balm with sunscreen to protect them. It makes me want to kiss them, which would be the opposite of protecting her in any way.

"What's that?" She nods at my hand.

"Oh. I brought you a new bottle of olive oil."

"I may have oversold how much I use that stuff. I haven't even come close to using up what you already gave me."

"No, I didn't think you'd be out yet. This one's a limited batch. Thought you might like to try it." I hold it out for her to take.

"Aw, I love the tiny olive branches embossed on the bottle. It will make such a cute little bud vase after the oil's all gone."

The bottle itself has delighted her, but I know the words on the label that indicate the quality and the rareness of this oil won't mean anything to her. I want to explain it all in intricate detail, to teach her everything I know about it. I swallow the urge to drown her in facts that wouldn't matter to her the way they do to me.

"Wait until you taste what's inside it."

"I've got a brand-new loaf of sourdough. Wanna come in and help me eat it?"

"You bake sourdough?"

"No. I buy sourdough." She opens her door. "From a very good bakery, and they just baked it this morning."

"I'd have to be crazy to walk away now." I follow her into her apartment and am instantly enveloped in a feeling of familiarity. Comfort. "Your place smells nice. I meant to tell you that when I was here last time."

"Thanks." She looks down as she opens the bread bag. "I guess between me being obnoxious and your mission of mercy on my fridge, there was never a good moment to mention my aromatherapy."

"Sorry if I was rude about your expired groceries."

"I'm sorry I had so many things that were expired."

"You weren't obnoxious, by the way."

She lays a few slices of sourdough on a plate. "Should I pop these in the toaster?"

"Do you have a pan?"

"Surprisingly, I have more than one."

"Got one large enough to grill two slices at the same time?"

She presents me with a perfectly sized pan. "Do you want butter?"

"No need. We have olive oil."

I set the pan over medium heat on her stovetop and drizzle a little of the oil from her future bud vase onto the surface. The slices lay side-by-side, soaking up the oil as the pan heats.

"Do you want garlic powder?"

"Nope. You need to taste the oil with no distractions." I bite back my thoughts on the sacrilege of using garlic powder with oil instead of fresh garlic.

"Huh. I've always considered garlic more of an enhancement than a distraction."

"This oil needs no enhancement. And I'm not sure you've ever actually had garlic."

She reaches into a small basket next to the stove and brings up a bulb. It might be a little past its prime, but it hasn't sprouted yet, and there's no denying it's real.

"Sometimes, even I prefer the real thing."

I'm sure she didn't mean that to sound suggestive. That doesn't make it any easier to leave all the flirty and dirty responses in my head unsaid. I manage it.

She wasn't trying to flirt, just proving she has real garlic. Nothing sexy about that.

For most people. But she made garlic a little sexy without even trying. I don't think she was trying. Maybe she was? Maybe now she thinks I'm too slow to pick up on innuendo. But if she didn't mean it that way and I'd said the first filthy thing that popped into my head . . .

"Don't you think you should flip those?"

"Not yet. They need a little longer." I wait less than two seconds before I flip the slices in the pan, drizzling a bit more oil under each one.

"Anything to keep from taking someone else's suggestion, huh?"

"What? They needed a few more seconds, that's all."

"You're the expert. Do we want cheese? I have some good parm. The real stuff, I promise. No can."

I stare at her silently as I remove the perfectly grilled slices of sourdough from the pan and return them to the plate.

"Just the oil," she says.

"Just the oil. I will take a small bowl if you've got one, though."

She hands me a cereal bowl, and I try not to laugh.

"My kitchen's not exactly equipped for gourmet tastings. I don't have any fancy little bowls for oils and sauces."

"This one's fine. I don't suppose you happen to have a silicone brush?"

She's the one staring in silence this time.

"We'll dip instead," I concede.

"I prefer to dip."

"That's handy since you don't own a basting brush."

"I'd still dip."

I tear a piece from one of the bread slices, dunk it into the oil, and lift it to her mouth. I know even as I'm doing it that this is too provocative, and I should've let her handle her own dipping and biting, but the chance to feed her is too enticing.

Her mouth opens for me as soon as I bring the bread to her lips. Her teeth sink into the warm, chewy bread, and oil drips down the side of my hand. It coats her mouth and her chin, and the way I want to spread it down her graceful neck and onto her chest is a clear confirmation I should not be here.

"Mmmm," she moans. Not at all helpful for my current condition. "Wow, that is so good. I could lick that off my enemies."

Never wanted so badly to be foe more than friend. "What part of your enemies?"

She wipes her mouth with her delicate fingers, again not abating my arousal by any means. Her cheeks pinken, and she rubs her slickened lips together. My brain forgets how to communicate with my lungs for a moment.

With my breath still held hostage, I watch as her fingertip swirls through the olive oil in the bowl. She traces my lips, letting the excess oil drip into my beard. My hand roughly captures her wrist, and my tongue claims the oil left on her skin, sparking a shiver down her spine. It's not cold in here.

I don't want to be her enemy, but I'm damn sure not feeling particularly heroic. Even the cadence of my pulse feels dangerous, and I'm positive her vibe isn't damsel in distress right now. Her eyes follow my free hand to the bowl where I rock two fingers back and forth through the oil, letting it run down my arm as I breach her mouth again.

"You should try it without the bread."

She sucks my fingers farther into her mouth, and her soft tongue glides back and forth over them the same way they disrupted the oil.

When she pulls her mouth away, she says, "Maybe we should try it on other body parts."

"Now that you mention it, the flavor of the oil does enhance different things in unique ways."

"I'm all for unique experiences."

I pick up the bottle and lead her down the hall by her wrist that's still in my grasp. She follows with gentle but willing steps, and I don't pull. Don't rush.

Inside her room, I release her wrist. I'm no longer guessing at her intentions. They're coming through clearly, and I don't plan to leave her dissatisfied.

Her bikini strings are stiff from the chlorine in the pool, but they still slide easily when I pull. First the one at her back, and then the one behind her neck. The light is off in the room but her mouth and chin glisten in the sunlight slanting through the partially-opened blinds. It casts slender striped shadows over her body.

They look like elongated piano keys. I give her the bottle to free both my hands. My fingers rest against the light and dark spaces on her warm ribcage, sliding to her back before I pull her closer, pressing rhythmically into her body. I'm not following a pattern, just reveling in the way her softness gives under my fingers that long to feel every inch of her.

She shimmies and domes her shoulders a little. I've tickled her without meaning to, but she doesn't pull away.

"Open the oil."

The way she follows that order without hesitation, her head tilted upward, eyes trained on mine until mine shift to watch her twist the lid . . . it's the sexiest thing I've ever seen.

"Fill the cap."

Again, she obeys.

"Pour it slowly over your chest."

She tips the cap and lets the oil fall in a thin stream, moving it slowly over her chest until it's all spilled onto her.

My hands glide gently, though not without great restraint, to meet the oil that's gently cascading toward her breasts. I pull it down to coat them from the top swells, around the sides, and upward from the bottom curves, purposely avoiding her nipples.

When her nipples are all that remain uncoated, only then do I spread my thumbs to graze over them, dragging the oil across the stiff peaks. She shivers again, and the piano keys distort in the sunlit sheen and shadows.

My oil-slicked hand unties her skirt. It falls to the rug, and I use both hands to slide her bottoms down her legs. She steps out of them and stands naked before me. The sun slices brighter through the blinds as clouds roll away beyond the rooftops.

I feel clouds rolling away inside me as well. My need for her burns too hot to hide from anymore.

Her hand slides into my hair when I lower my mouth to her nipple. She pulls slightly to pause me. "I should've showered. At least rinsed the chlorine off my body."

Shaking my head, I smile up at her. "No, this is exactly right just the way we are."

The subtle smile on her face is beautiful, but the lust in her eyes is the goddamn holy grail I didn't come here to find. Subconsciously, maybe I did. Consciously, even—if I were willing to admit it—but it doesn't matter. All that matters is that she's mine right now.

My tongue swirls over her hard nipple, tasting first the green grassy notes of the oil on the tip, followed by the nutty sweetness as my tongue flattens. Buttery and rich. The faint salty tang of her sweat and chlorine rises, giving way to a hint of bitterness as I suck harder.

As my mouth works, alternately drawing her nipple deeper and laving my tongue over it as it swells, the notes all comingle, and there is nothing in a bottle anywhere on earth that compares.

Ellis whimpers, and I pull her closer, letting my hands roam down to cup and squeeze her ass. I walk her toward the bed, and free her nipple to ask, "How willing are you to risk oil stains on your comforter?"

"Ruin it. I'll think about this moment every time I look at it."

I take the bottle from her and pour a generous amount into my hand. The feel of it heating between my hand and her body as I rub it down her back and over her ass is pure delicious sin.

When I move to her front and slide my slippery hand down the middle of her torso, I don't stop to distribute it evenly. I keep going until her soft pussy is under my palm and I'm kneading and slicking her there as I watch her chest heave.

Her stomach tightens when I slip a finger inside her, and then her satiny walls clench to claim my second finger.

The relaxing of her abdomen travels up to her shoulders. Her whole body softens while I continue to explore it, except her pussy that tightens even as her juices flow around my fingers. Her arousal and the oil combine, wafting an intoxicating scent between us. I need to taste her. Just her first . . .

I return the bottle to her, step back and toe off my shoes, pull my shirt over my head, and then push my shorts down until I can kick them off, too. I nod toward the bottle and then the nightstand to indicate she should set it there.

"No more?" she asks.

"Not yet. Sit on the edge of the bed and lie back."

"Wouldn't you prefer me to be all the way on the bed so you can be more comfortable?"

"No. I'd prefer to be on my knees with your feet on my shoulders and your legs butterflied open shamelessly while my mouth does depraved things to your sweet little snatch. Tongue. Teeth. I want you to buck and squirm until tears leak from your eyes and you make sounds you've never heard leaving your own mouth and your pussy flows like a fountain all over my face. And when that's done, then we'll add some oil and do it all over again."

"Where did this version of you come from?"

"Italy."

Our laughter arrives on choppy breaths, hoarse and unsteady, but together.

The Awkward After

Ellis

THIS IS WHY I love a man with a beard, the soft feel of it on my inner thighs . . . against my pussy as his mouth closes in. Malcolm's beard is exceptionally soft.

I bet his shower has a trio of matching bottles: shampoo, conditioner, and bodywash all in the same scent from the same high-end product line.

And there's undoubtedly a small, dark glass bottle of beard oil on his counter. He's a products guy, and I'm so going to give him shit about it later. But right now, I'm going to reap the benefits with pleasure.

His hands squeeze my thighs while he holds them open. It's not like I'm going to close my legs with his tongue circling my opening and moving up to barely graze around my clit like this, getting just close enough to almost make my back arch before he teases lower again.

I've said more times than I can count that I prefer a man with rough hands because I don't want anyone who's gentle in bed, but I think now that I may have drawn a false correlation. Malcolm's soft hands have me pinned exactly where he wants me.

And he might not have been overstating the things he predicted his mouth could make me do.

My juices have already soaked his beard, and it's cold now when it touches my delicate skin, but only for a moment before his warm breath blankets over the chill. The contrasting sensation causes my glutes to clench and my hips to tilt, even as they miraculously loosen further to let my legs fall wider.

I'm flexible, but this is a whole new level. I think he's melted my tendons. My legs are disconnected from my body. Putty in his hands. All of me.

He pushes two fingers inside my pussy as his tongue focuses on my clit exclusively. My hips lift and rock when he slides his fingers back and forth the way he did in the oil earlier. The vision of that oil running down his hand has my arousal following the same path.

I feel the promise of his teeth as he buries his face deeper between my languid legs, abandoning my clit again. It throbs in the absence of his mouth, and I need him to go back to it, but he denies me as I rock faster, riding his face. Shamelessly. Another prophesy fulfilled.

His tongue flicks around his fingers, tasting me again, and then it joins them on the next thrust, probing me harder and faster. There is nothing gentle about the way he's treating me.

My regards to Italy.

I'm vaguely aware of the needy moans leaving my mouth when he returns to my clit. He isn't gentle there anymore either.

He tongues my swollen clit until my breath stutters, and then he sucks it, stealing my breath. My core heats and my fingers sink into his hair as a tightening contraction overtakes my body.

The warmth intensifies until it sets off a chain reaction of sparks. All the air in my lungs rushes out at the first jolt of my orgasm, pulling with it a scream.

I'm not a screamer. But he knew I could be. He was sure he could make me make sounds I'd never made with anyone else. He has impulse control now, but it's come with an arrogance that I wish I didn't like so much.

My legs shake as he releases them and stands. I can barely control my muscles well enough to reposition myself on the bed.

He slides his arms under my body and lifts me from the mattress, turning me and setting me back down with my head on a pillow.

I roll to my side to watch him free his erection, and my eyes go straight to the glistening crown already coated in his precum.

No one who knows us would imagine the two of us here like this, naked in the glow of early afternoon sun. Sober, yet drunk on desire.

Nothing about this feels strange, though.

His eyes drink in my post-orgasm body: skin flushed, nipples hard, eyes probably radiating just how likely I am to do whatever he wants . . .

"What about round two with the oil?" I ask.

He reaches for the bottle and removes the cap. "I'm glad to see you're developing a taste for the real thing."

The mattress dips under his weight, and I slide closer to him, holding out my cupped hand. "Let me put it on you this time."

His body quakes as my request registers. Tipping the bottle slowly, he lets the oil pool in my palm.

I reach down to coat his dick, and he quakes again when my fingers close against it. The feel of satiny skin stretched over a hard cock is one of my favorite things, but adding oil to it elevates it exponentially. Lube isn't the same. This oil warms instantly and it's the perfect consistency to create an easy glide, but I can still feel our skin-to-skin contact.

It highlights, doesn't mask.

When I lower my head to his ribcage and slide down his side, continuing to stroke him, he grips the back of my neck hard enough to stop me. "I offered you a round two with the oil."

"You can owe me. I want to taste it on you." I rub my slick hand up his inner thigh, stopping just shy of his balls. Looking up into his eyes, I ask, "Deal?"

"I didn't come here to argue."

Swirling my tongue over his crown, I want to work him into the same type of frenzy he did me, but I also just plain want him, and I've never been one to deny my own longings and curiosities.

He groans when I lick the thick vein on the underside from the base to the tip. I close my mouth over the head and let my tongue map every detail as I move down his shaft. The taste of the oil alternates between herbaceous and sweet to pungent and bitter, smooth to sharp and back again, until all the notes blend into an enticing combination that I want to taste again and again.

I want to be able to single out the flavors distinctly the way I tasted them before, but I realize I won't be able to do that until the next time I taste it fresh. They can't be separated once they've become one, but I already want to taste it again for the first time so I can appreciate it more and notice the things I missed.

This is how cravings develop.

Malcolm's thighs lock, and I realize his release is building.

I pull my mouth off his delicious cock with my cheeks slightly suctioned to torment him a little, and lick my lips while I stare up at him. "Tasty."

His smile is strained. "Your tasting skills are unmatched."

"Those are the least of my skills."

His smirk says *prove it*, but his dick jerks believingly beneath me as I straddle him.

The way his big hands clutch my hips is assertive. He's not going to let me be in charge here, and I don't mind relinquishing as much control as he wants to take.

He guides me onto his cock, watching through hooded eyes when his stiff, slick hard-on enters me, grunting softly while it disappears inch-by-inch as I slowly slide down to take it.

Having a man watch as my pussy stretches to take him turns me on. Having this man watch it happen makes me feel like a goddess.

I rock forward and back like I'm riding on a wave. He clasps his hands behind his head and continues to watch the way our bodies join, the way mine moves on him. My eyes spot the olive oil bottle propped against my pillow. I never noticed when he put it there, but I reach for it now, and his eyes follow my hand.

Not bothering to fill the cap this time, I let the oil stream freely from the bottle onto my breasts. Malcolm draws a deep breath as I spread it over my body with one hand. Leaning forward again, I nestle the half-empty bottle back against the pillow, setting the cap loosely on top but not bothering to tighten it.

Sitting up straight with his cock buried to the hilt inside me, I use both hands to distribute the oil, pulling it up and across my chest, and then down my torso.

He moans when my hands return to my tits.

I pluck at my slippery nipples, watching as my fingers lose contact, leaving my hard peaks shining in the dim light. The clouds move again and new shadows flicker over my body, prompting me to move again, too.

His hands follow mine as I gain momentum, fucking him by instinct now, no more performative moves.

My palms rest on my thighs, working to pump faster on him, and I let my head fall back, pushing my chest forward.

He plays with my nipples, pinching harder to try to hold on longer, but the oil rejects his grip, forcing his fingers off each time he tries.

A burn builds in my quads, but I feel his dick swell and lurch inside me, and there is no way I'm slowing down when he's this close.

His voice ruptures the silence we've fallen into. "Damn, you know how to work that tight little pussy."

"I'm working your big hard cock," I correct, teasing him.

"You're doing it right."

"I aim to please."

"Your skills are once again unmatched."

"Did you think I was too much of a good girl to fuck you right?"

"I never doubted you for a minute. But you are a very good girl."

"Sometimes I'm bad. A brat, even."

"I love it even more when a good girl's bad." He flips us and drives his cock balls-deep into me with one thrust. "You can be a brat with me anytime, as long as you know what that'll get you."

"What will it get me?"

"It'll get your pretty little ass spanked."

"How hard?"

"Hard enough to leave my red handprint on your skin."

He fucks me in hard, rhythmic thrusts that force my hips off the mattress and yelps from my mouth. "That wouldn't change me."

"But would it make you happy? To have a man know exactly how much pain you needed? And when?"

"Yes. Yes."

Fuck, I didn't mean to admit that to him.

My body trembles and my hips rock up while my thighs attempt to draw closed against him. His name leaves my lips like a plea, betraying my control as I come all over his dick—shamelessly, and with my eyes leaking. A surrender as involuntary as breathing, but complete. More complete than I'm prepared to face.

I've given him everything he said I would: the bucking and squirming and sounds, and now, the tears that aren't crying. They are a dam bursting that I can't hold back.

He can't hold back any longer either, but his release definitely does not come with tears. His jaw locks and his involuntary sounds fill my bedroom as he lets go.

"I get it now," I whisper.

"Get what?"

"The eroticism of olive oil." My laughter is weak, but only because all of me is weak.

"Good." He kisses me softly. "But I won't be happy until I've shown you the romance of it, too."

We're still talking about olive oil, right?

I see the small bottle that made this whole encounter possible—fallen onto its side, spilling its contents onto my bed. It's too late to save it. There's barely any left.

"Oh, no. Looks like we lost the rest of the oil."

Malcolm grabs the bottle and rights it, but realizes immediately it's all gone.

"I have to admit, this has been the best way possible to enjoy a cute, little sixty-dollar bottle of extra virgin," he says, smiling and dropping the bottle as if it's no big deal. "Worth every penny we spilled."

I nearly choke on my tongue. "How much? Are you serious? For that little bottle?"

"Don't worry. I get a discount." He winks.

"I cannot believe we just wasted an oil that costs that much."

"Wasted is definitely not the word I would use for what we did with that oil."

I probably laugh too long at that comment, but we're headed for the *awkward after*, and I don't know what else to do. There was nothing uncomfortable about having sex with him, but the discomfort is closing in quickly now.

Lying naked in my bed with Malcolm—both of us covered in oil, no less—I can't tell if he's feeling the strangeness of it yet. He won't stop staring at me. And smiling.

The smile on my face can't be tamed either, but there's so much anxiety brewing behind it.

Was this a mistake? It didn't feel like one, but there's something uncertain roiling inside me.

"What time is it?" I ask.

He reaches for his watch on my nightstand. I don't remember him putting it there, but I guess it's a good thing he took it off before things got too oily.

"3:33. Make a wish."

I close my eyes. "I wish I didn't have to have dinner at my parents' tonight."

"Oh, yeah. I forgot about that."

"You're coming, too?" My stomach somersaults. How am I supposed to sit across from him in my parents' house and pretend I haven't sucked olive oil off his dick? My years of high school theater did not prepare me for that scene.

"No. I'm meeting Brody for drinks after. I haven't seen him since they got back from their honeymoon."

"He's smart. Meeting you gives him an excuse to duck out at a certain time." As soon as I've said it, I realize how bad it sounds. "I mean, not that he wouldn't rather have drinks with you. That came out wrong."

"No worries. I get it. If you need an escape, you can say you're coming, too. You don't really have to come if you don't want to, but you can tell your parents you're coming out with us. Not that you can't come. You totally can."

"Right. Because it's not going to be stressful enough just to have dinner with my brother after this. Why not add drinks with the two of you to top it off?"

"He won't suspect anything at dinner."

"No, but if you were there, he might. What if we can't help but look at each other weirdly now? Don't be weird around me, okay?"

"I promise not to be any weirder than usual."

"Thanks. I guess I can focus on Amanda, and let her tell me all about Italy. I assume you gave them some travel tips?"

"Told them all the best places to go."

"Were they all olive orchards?"

He flinches like I've slapped him. "Not all of them."

We laugh together again, and I realize none of my anxiety is about being alone with him after what we've done. It's all about going back out into the world.

It's not like people will take one look at me and know. He didn't brand me with his company logo.

Or even his handprint.

I can feel my face turning red at that thought. There is no way I can be around him and my brother (or my parents) at the same time ever again.

But what about just him? There's no reason anybody else has to know if we don't want them to.

"Just so you know," I say, pausing to take a breath before the rest of my admission. "I don't have any regrets about this afternoon."

"I don't either. What are the chances we can do it again?"

"They might be better than average." My cheeks flush at this, too.

"And if I wanted to buy you dinner first next time?"

"You mean, like a date?"

"Yes. Exactly like that."

"Dating would be complicated for us."

"Easy is overrated."

"Maybe we should grab a shower and hold off an any rash decisions."

"Wait a minute. I can fuck you and shower with you, but taking you to dinner would be too bold?"

"You know my reasons, Malcolm."

"This can't be a sex only deal, Ellis. I want to spend time with you with your clothes on, too."

"So, you want to skip the shower then?" In my heart, I know this isn't the time to be cute, but I'm not ready for this conversation. I'm the one who wanted to hurry things along when he was pumping the brakes, but I need a minute.

"No. I'm going to soap up every inch of your gorgeous body until I've washed away all traces of oil. And me. You're going to have a lovely dinner with your family tonight. But Wednesday night, you're dining with me. We'll keep the oil on the table, but there will be traces of me left on you when the sun comes up on Thursday."

"You don't get to decide that."

"If you want a say in any of this, you're going to have to participate." He stands and pulls me to my feet. "But right now, it's time to hit the shower, Buttercup."

Unforgettable
Malcolm

THE FEEL OF HER soapy body under my hands is almost as good as when it was coated in olive oil. She's letting me wash away the oil like I promised. My legs are weak, but I could stand here and do this for hours.

Pushing me away gently, she says, "I have to wash my hair."

"Let me do it."

"It's too thick. You won't get all the oil out."

"You have control issues."

"You mispronounced skills. I'll let you rinse it."

Washing the lather from her hair and watching the suds run down her back, I contemplate the old differences in our personalities: she was a free-spirit who struggled to meet her parents' expectations, but almost always managed to stay in control, and I was a loose cannon who had basically no self-control.

I've gained a lot. I'd love to help her let go of a little more.

It was practically an act of rebellion for her to choose the freelancing path. It's not the safe choice, and her accomplished parents are risk-averse to their very cores. Ellis has professional commitments and responsibilities, but she chooses them. I respect that so damn much.

But I suspect she still struggles to toe the line around her parents, feeling an ingrained need to make them proud. That means keeping parts of herself under wraps—the parts that bring her the most joy. I hate that, but even so, I respect her reasons.

I can't fault anyone for the way they navigate their family dynamics because I never had a family that gave a damn what I did with my life.

Hers is the closest I had, and truth be told, I shift into a different persona when I'm around her parents now, one that's more guarded, careful not to be defensive, but never too re-laxed either. It's my business persona. Minus the personality. All business, none of the personal parts of me that actually make me successful.

After years of being their son's unfortunate—sometimes to the point of being embarrassing—choice for a best friend, I still feel the need to prove my worth. Sometimes my success feels like a big fuck-you to them and everyone else who doubted me.

And I'll always wish it didn't. I wish it could just feel like mine with no axes to grind.

Someday.

Ellis pulls away to put conditioner in her hair. It smells botanical, but not floral. The scent is fresh, and it reminds me of an olive orchard during the harvest, the leaves perfuming the air with the green, herbal notes that are more prevalent after the flowers have faded. The blossoms that die off leave nothing behind, but those that become fruit take on a new, stronger scent. One that is unforgettable once you've smelled it.

With her hair slicked back, water glistening on her cheek, and tiny droplets clinging to the edges of her lashes before they fall, she looks too beautiful to be real. She'd flick soap in my eyes if I told her so. I say it with a kiss instead.

Back in her room to get dressed, I notice a picture on her dresser that I didn't see before. It's her with her hair slicked back, water glistening on her cheeks, and tiny droplets clinging to her lashes, but she's not in a shower.

She's emerging from sparkling turquoise water. It's not a pool. An ocean. Tropical? Mediterranean?

I pick it up for a closer look. "Where was this picture taken?"

"The Maldives. My college graduation gift."

"Ah, the trip. Brody went to Spain."

"Brody went to party. I went to be a mermaid."

My eyebrows lift questioningly. "To feel like a mermaid or to perform as one?"

"A little of both." She lifts another framed picture from her dresser. "See the blond in the middle of this shot? That's Sedona Rain. She's a famous mermaid."

She stares at me as if she expects me to make fun of what she's said and she's waiting for me to get it out of my system.

"And she lives in the Maldives?"

"No. But she held a mermaid boot camp there the year I graduated with my business degree to please my parents. I wasn't proud when I crossed that stage. I felt like I'd wasted time I should've spent pursuing my real goals. Sedona's event was elite. You had to apply and be accepted. I never thought I'd get in, but I did. And I completed every challenge while I was there. When I got on the plane to come home, I finally felt proud. Every time I look at these photos, I remember that feeling."

"I'm shocked your parents went along with that."

"They have no idea why I chose the Maldives."

"You never told them what you did while you were there?"

"Nope."

"Did they let you go alone?"

"Oh, no. Are you kidding? They paid for Maren to go, too. Bootcamp was five days. The trip was for ten. We had a fucking blast."

Once again, we both laugh, and it feels so natural. So right.

"And then I came home and enrolled in an esthetician course and a theatrical makeup academy at the same time. Told my parents if they wouldn't pay for it, I'd take out loans."

"I bet their jaws were clenched when they made those payments."

"They never paid a dime."

"Damn. I'm sorry."

"Don't be. Spite is a powerful motivator."

"I know that truth all too well."

"And now you know a little more about me."

"Yeah."

"Not scared off yet, huh?"

"No. You don't scare me, Ellis. You intrigue me."

"Like a freak show?"

"Pfft. Like a smoke show."

Her eye roll is dramatic as she sets the frames back in place on her dresser. But I see her smile before I pull her in for a hug. She hides her face against my chest, and I kiss the top of her head.

She smells unforgettable.

Ad Blocker

Ellis

THANKFULLY, BRODY AND AMANDA have nine-thousand photographs from Italy and a story to go with each one. It makes dinner take a lot longer, but also lessens the pain of being asked if I've found a better health insurance plan yet, if I have steady work lined up, and the worst, if I'm seeing anyone.

Oof.

My hand fidgets with Malcolm's watch in the pocket of my sweatshirt. I noticed it on my nightstand as I was walking out the door and grabbed it so I could give it to Brody, since he's seeing him right after dinner.

And then the weight of that bad idea hit me like a brick to the face.

How the hell would I explain why I had Malcolm's watch? I damn sure couldn't say he left it on my nightstand. In a moment of panic, I shoved it in my pocket.

My thumb traces the thick gold bezel as Amanda tells us how shocked she was when she ordered a latte in Florence and got a glass of milk. She goes on to explain how she should've asked for a caffè latte instead.

I love her, but honestly, how to order coffee seems like the sort of basic thing one should learn before going to another country. Coffee is too important to risk.

My tolerance is unusually low for everything right now. I've eaten plenty, yet somehow, my internal reactions are hangry. I think I'm managing to keep my surly thoughts to myself until Brody gives me the big brother look.

It's a look he's given me since I hit puberty. It says I need to check my attitude. I haven't even said anything!

To be fair, I am aware my face sometimes says a lot, even when I keep my mouth shut. The last thing I want to do is be rude to Amanda. She's so excited to share all these stories, and I'm genuinely happy for them.

But I'm so ready to leave. I had a tiring afternoon. Plus, I should really return Malcolm's watch. It looks expensive. What if I lose it? I'd never forgive myself.

We exchanged numbers before he left my apartment. I'll just text him and tell him to meet me before he heads to the bar. Easy enough.

I'm suddenly aware of Brody's fingers snapping in front of my face. My hand squeezes his fingers as tightly as I can. "Do not snap at me."

"Well, pay attention. We're trying to invite you to go grab a drink with us."

"A drink?" *Oh, no, that won't be happening.*

"Yeah. We're meeting Malcolm. I know he always got on your nerves, but you haven't been around him in years. He was so shocked when he saw you at the wedding. I think he was expecting you to still be a teenager. Y'all should get to know each other as adults."

Excuse me!

"What? Why?"

"Because he was like your second big brother growing up. And he doesn't have any siblings besides us. Come on. Be a good little sister and come get to know your other brother again. You might be surprised how much you like him now."

Every cell in my body cringes. He is not my other brother. Not in any way, shape or form. And I am well aware how much I like him now.

"I never thought of him as a second brother. He was just your obnoxious friend."

"Well, he's not so obnoxious anymore. And he definitely thinks of you like a sister. Just one drink. Come on."

I can assure everyone in this room that Malcolm most definitely does not think of me as a sister. Except I can't, actually.

Mom shifts in her chair. "Ellis, be nice. Even if you don't want to see Malcolm, you could go have a drink with your brother and your new sister-in-law."

Now she's giving me the mom look.

Dad sighs the way he always does when I'm *being difficult.*

"Okay, fine." I turn to Amanda. "I'm sure you already know this, but my reluctance to go to the bar with y'all has absolutely nothing to do with you. You are a gift, and I don't know what my overbearing brother ever did to deserve you."

Brody laughs as if I'm joking.

"I promise not to ramble on about our honeymoon in the bar." Amanda drops her phone into her purse. "But I'm so happy you're coming with us. We haven't hung out in forever."

"Seriously, one drink. I have to work in the morning."

"Tomorrow's Sunday," my dad says. "If you had a real job, you wouldn't have to work again until Monday."

"Thanks for your input, Dad. I'll tell Malcolm you said hi."

"Tell him they're selling extra virgin olive oil in dollar stores now. Friend of mine is a manager in the investment department at Chase Bank. I can probably get him an interview."

"I'll let Brody tell him that."

My brother and I exchange a look all our own: the look of sibling solidarity.

Malcolm is already at the bar when we arrive. He holds up his full beer in salute, so I assume he hasn't been here long. When he sees me standing next to Amanda, he looks surprised. I flash an expression that I hope conveys this wasn't my idea.

Maybe my being here won't make this hard for him. He doesn't seem fazed by much these days. Meanwhile, my stomach feels like one of those giant clear inflatable balls that people climb into and run across parks. Except the tiny people in my stomach are stuck running in place, rolling the ball over and over again and getting nowhere.

"Ellis," he says when we reach him. "It's good to see you again." He leans in for a hug, and I linger a few seconds too long, just in case he needs to whisper something in my ear.

Like what, I don't know.

Get the fuck out of here? Meet me in the bathroom in five minutes?

While my brain continues to generate increasingly inappropriate possibilities, he releases me and turns to hug my brother and Amanda. He immediately asks about some olive orchards and mills he made them promise to check out.

The ball in my stomach stops turning as I wait for their response. All I can think is that they better have gone to those places. And taken pictures. And they better say how much they enjoyed every minute of it. That it was everything he said it would be. I don't care if they hated the whole experience. It's really fucking important to him, and if they shit on his passion, I swear I will . . .

What? What will I do? Make a scene? No. I'll stand here and swallow my anger until the tiny people in my stomach riot amongst themselves because that's the only sane option.

Thankfully, Amanda pulls up pictures on her phone and gushes about how incredible each place was. Brody tells Malcolm everyone they met at each stop raved about him like he was a celebrity.

Malcolm laughs and shakes his head. "What are y'all drinking?"

"You buying?" Brody asks.

"Only for the ladies. You're on your own tab."

"Fuck you, man. My dad wants you to know he saw extra virgin olive oil in a dollar store. If you're interested in working at Chase Bank, he has a contact."

"Thank god for Gary."

We all laugh at that.

He doesn't seem mad at all. I'm still stewing on my dad's comment when I said I had to work tomorrow.

A table opens up after we get our drinks, and Brody and Amanda lead the way. I take the opportunity to surreptitiously pass Malcolm's watch to him.

He smiles and slips it onto his wrist, fastening it as I step in front of him to take my seat.

"When did you put that watch on?" Amanda asks immediately.

Damn, their kids aren't going to get away with shit. She doesn't miss a beat.

Malcolm clears his throat and scoots his chair closer to the table. "I took it off to wash my hands in the bathroom before y'all got here. Just remembered it was in my pocket and put it back on so I don't lose it."

"You took your watch off to wash your hands?" Brody asks. "Were you scrubbing up for surgery?"

"I wasn't going to tell you, but I sold your kidneys on the dark web an hour ago. You're going to start to feel very sleepy in a few minutes. When you wake up, you'll be in a tub of ice."

"As his spouse, I demand half the proceeds." Amanda points an accusatory finger at Malcolm. "One of those kidneys is mine."

"I'm feeling the love over here." Brody takes a drink of his beer.

They're all such good friends. I have a separate relationship with each of them, but in the group, I'm the outsider. Even if Malcolm and I did start to date, I'd have to act like the outsider when we were all together. Unless we told them.

I watch my brother's face as they all continue to joke, and I imagine his reaction to that news. I can see the curve of his smile straighten. His eyes narrow. His jaw tightens, and the veins in his neck bulge.

I'd be the wrecking ball to their friendship. Moments like this wouldn't happen anymore. I always thought Malcolm needed Brody growing up. Maybe he did, but now I can see that Brody needs him, too. They're not both my brothers, but they're brothers to each other.

Amanda would be caught in the middle, but she loves Brody. She'd be loyal to him. Everyone would lose so much. And for what? Malcolm and I don't even know each other.

"I hate to have to cut out so early, but I have to work tomorrow." I stand hurriedly.

"You didn't even finish your drink," Amanda says.

Malcolm's eyes plead with me to stay. I hate that I think I can read his fucking eyes. For all I actually know, that look means he's glad I'm leaving. I can't just see what I want to see here.

"Please, don't let it go to waste." I push my glass toward Amanda.

Malcolm stands and embraces me more fully than when we arrived. This time he does whisper in my ear. "I'll call you later."

How loud was that? I swear it echoed in my head. Brody and Amanda are both looking at me, but not in shock or anger, so they must not have heard him.

I give Brody a side hug as he remains seated. "You know," he says. "If you had a real job—"

I punch him in the shoulder, and then I blow a kiss to Amanda.

"Wait!" she says. "I'll walk you out."

"No, you don't need to do that."

"Yes, she does," Brody says.

"We got you something in Italy, but we had it shipped home, and it just came in today."

"That's really sweet. I can't believe you bought me a present on your honeymoon."

"We couldn't resist it. I'm so excited to give it to you."

The moment we're outside, she says, "Okay, could you feel Malcolm's eyes on you?"

"I didn't feel anything. I think he's probably just still shocked that I'm grown." I laugh nervously. "Like Brody said."

"Brody's your brother. That may be all he heard when Malcolm mentioned you the other day, but we were in the car and the phone was on Bluetooth. I know what I heard in his voice."

"Stop. Brody would kill us both. Anyway, Malcolm is like my second brother."

"Nice try, but you already said earlier you don't see him that way. Brody would be fine. He might explode a little at first, but that's what he does. He'd adjust, trust me. You're single. Malcolm's single. You're both grown now. Do what you want."

"Oh, I will. Just not with Malcolm. He's not really my type."

"What exactly is it about him that you object to? His amazing job? His great sense of humor? He's handsome. And he's kind and honest. Well-traveled and open-minded." She pulls a giftbag loaded with pillowy layers of tissue from the backseat. Her eyebrows waggle, and as she hands me the bag she says, "Excellent beard."

"Okay, that's enough." I hold up my hand. "This is me, blocking all ads for Malcolm."

"I'll put them on pause. Open it here. I want to see your reaction."

"Okay." I toss the tissue paper back into their car as I yank it out of the bag. That'll drive Brody crazy, which adds a whole other level to this gift. The box reveals a clear plastic window as I lift it from the bag. Inside is the most beautiful blown-glass mermaid. Her tail is all opalescent shades of green that swirl over every scale. I tilt the box and watch the colors change. "Amanda, she's gorgeous. I want to take her out and hold her, but I'm scared I'll drop her."

"Take her out when you get home. I just wanted to be sure you liked it."

"I love it. So much." I hug her, feeling more thankful than ever that Brody brought her into my life.

She really doesn't miss a thing, but she's completely wrong in thinking it would be fine if I dated Malcolm.

I know my brother. He would lose his shit, blow up his best friendship, never look at me the same again . . . it would be awful.

And Malcolm would be destroyed. Nothing is worth that.

I'm certainly not.

Amanda is right about one thing: Malcolm's great. He'll find someone equally great who won't wreak havoc on his friendships. They'll all meet for drinks every week. And I'll be a Fantasia Faerie. We will all get what we need.

If he ever asks about me, Brody will say I'm fine, still doing that ridiculous mermaid thing. Amanda will shove his shoulder and tell him to be nice.

And because she's so kind, she'll never tell me if she thinks I made a mistake. All ads for Malcolm will be forever muted.

Thieves in the Night
Malcolm

I LOSE MY BALANCE and hop off my board, trying to dodge a speeding Maserati as I approach the center of the crosswalk. The sign says WALK, which also implies it's safe to roll, but that asshole just careened around the corner without ever looking.

A group of pedestrians stands stunned in the crosswalk, trying to catch their breath after our shared seven a.m. brush with vehicular manslaughter.

"I hope your fucking transmission falls out!" I yell with a middle finger salute while I run after my skateboard that's slammed itself against a storm drain.

Screaming obscenities in the street is the kind of thing I generally try to avoid. There are families walking around here all the time. Also, the media is still interested in my quirks. I'd rather not go from eccentric to raving lunatic in a single headline.

I'd been doing so good since I woke up this morning, not obsessing about how Ellis didn't answer my call after I left the bar Saturday night. Barely even wondering if she'd bothered to listen to my voicemail. Not at all feeling offended that she'd read both my texts yesterday and hasn't responded to either one.

Thanks to Mr. Fuckface Maserati, I'm pissed off about all those things now on top of his shitty driving. And I've got anger to spare. This is probably not the best time to log on and check the emails I ignored all weekend. I'm pissed off about having done that, too.

What's the point in avoiding work all weekend if your social life isn't even going to benefit?

Safely inside in my office with a cup of steaming black coffee, I steady myself to brave my inbox, and turn all my news and market notifications back on. My eyes erratically scan the headlines that are popping off like fireworks on my screen. And then the details.

Houston Warehouse Heist. Luxury Olive Oil. Estimated Value of $2.5 Million. Premium Brand. Approximately 20 Truckloads. 300 Pallets. Over 200,000 Bottles.

I make the call that I know won't yield the answers I want, but I have to hear it for myself. Nico doesn't bother with hello.

"I've been expecting your call for hours."

"I am already aware I've lost a lot of oil in this, Nico, but please tell me the most important pallet had shipped already. Tell me it's sitting at the fulfillment center, and I have nothing to worry about."

"Every bottle is trackable. They're being traced. HPD will probably call you at some point today."

"I don't need to talk to the police. I need to know that my oil isn't lost to the black market! How the hell am I supposed to launch an olive oil subscription box without the featured oil for

my first box? I've promised promo boxes to influential people.
People with full schedules and deadlines who've given me their
time. People whose voices could make or break this venture. Tell
me you understand that!"

"All I can tell you is that our security cameras were working.
The police department has the footage. Our inventory tracking
system has a record of every lot number, and they've all been
given to the cops and the media."

"The media. Fuck me." I throw my glasses onto my desk and
squeeze the bridge of my nose. "An asshole in a Maserati almost
turned me into a greasy spot on the street this morning. In the
moment right after he passed and I realized everyone was safe, I
was stupid enough to feel lucky."

"Sometimes, ignorance is a blessing."

"That security footage better be a blessing. Can they read the
plates on the trucks?"

"Come on, Malcolm. You know these thieves weren't ama-
teurs. If there were plates on those trucks, they weren't valid.
Listen, I know you lost vital product, but you're not the only
one. The entire goddamn warehouse got wiped out. I've been
fielding phone calls like this all morning. I'm doing all I can over
here."

"You own the warehouse. Of course you're the one getting
the calls! I'm glad you've got good cameras, but that doesn't
change the fact that they got in. How did this happen? Twenty
fucking trucks? That shit took time, Nico."

"It was obviously a well-coordinated effort. And now, I'm trying to coordinate recovery efforts. I'll say it again. I'm doing all I can over here." He ends the call. No goodbye.

I've got a launch party happening in three months. The venue is booked. The fulfillment center is supposed to start sending out promo boxes in two weeks. Ads have been scheduled and paid for. Every stolen bottle is going to cost me time and money, but the one pallet that matters most can't be re-ordered.

Limited release. Special edition.

I look at the last remaining sample bottle sitting on my desk. All that remains from a box of 24 precious little bottles with embossed olives and leaves . . . my index finger traces around the curves. At least I put 22 samples into the hands of notable chefs.

They know they can trust me to source the best oil in the world. Those bottles will be put to good use.

But nothing will compare to the way I used that bottle with Ellis, and there's no one else I'd rather give this last one. She won't write about it or mention it in an interview or highlight it on a menu. She won't rave about it in an online video or during a segment on a talk show or a podcast.

The culinary world won't miss a mermaid's opinion, but I need to hear it. Hers is the only voice I want to hear right now. And she won't even reply to my texts.

I place the bottle on a bookshelf, safely away from the edge of my desk, and then I start reading my emails. I'm numb, but I'm functioning. Working is the best way to get through this.

Staying busy breeds solutions. When I'm idle, my mind goes to unproductive places sometimes.

At 4:30, a text from Ellis lights up my phone:

> *Just saw news about an olive oil heist. Hope that doesn't affect you.*

I laugh for the first time all day. It's the silver lining I didn't expect.

> *I am unfortunately very affected. You should let me come over and cook you dinner tonight. I have one last bottle of that limited release oil. You'll have a pair of matching bud vases.*

> ...

> ...

> ...

How many times is she going to start over?

> *I'll be there at five-thirty. We will use the oil on food only. I just want to share it with you again. Besides, you haven't tasted it on my couscous.*

> *Well, if there's going to be couscous! WTF is couscous?*

> *You'll love it. I'll bring wine, too.*

> *Pick one that comes in a bottle that would make a pretty vase.*

> *How else does anyone pick a wine? See you at five-thirty.*

"So, this is couscous, huh?" She examines the bowl of steaming grains as I squeeze fresh lemon juice over the top. When I sprinkle chopped parsley onto it, she smiles. "I love the way parsley smells."

"Me, too." I top it with a generous helping of shredded parmesan and drizzle the special oil onto it like I have a warehouse full of the stuff.

To use it sparingly would feel like letting the thieves win. There may not be much left, but I want to enjoy it with gusto, not sorrow. The way good things are meant to be savored.

I spoon the couscous onto our plates, and place what I hope is a perfectly cooked filet mignon on each one.

"There is nothing green on this plate." She shakes her head disapprovingly.

"You saw me put the parsley on the couscous. What color was that, again?"

"Parsley is not a vegetable."

"Try it."

She tentatively lifts a forkful of couscous and stares at it for a beat before she eats it.

I watch her tilt her head from side-to-side like she's contemplating the taste. She swallows, but I can't read her reaction.

"Is it supposed to be chewy?"

"A little."

"It owes a lot to the parsley. And that oil."

"We owe a lot to that oil, too."

"Yeah, I might be biased, but it's pretty good."

"That's exactly how I marketed it. Pretty good."

"You sell this one?"

I sigh. "I almost did."

"How do you almost sell something?"

"You import it and take orders for it, and then it gets stolen out of the warehouse before you can fulfill a single one."

"Wow. No wonder you're so successful. I bet nobody else has ever tried doing it like that."

"My methods are all my own."

She takes a drink of her wine. "I'm really sorry that happened, Malcolm."

"Thanks. How's the wine?"

"Pretty good."

"And the bottle?"

She shrugs. "It'll do."

A Sunflower in Every Bottle

Ellis

MALCOLM'S BEARD TICKLES MY jaw as he leans down to kiss me goodbye. He's not in bed with me. But he definitely spent the night.

Shit.

Why am I so bad at doing the right thing?

"What time is it?" I ask, trying not to sound annoyed that he's here. It's not him I'm upset with.

"Later than it should be. I've got to go home and shower. I need to make a dozen phone calls before lunch, and I have to talk to the police about the heist. I didn't take their call yesterday. If I don't sit down with them today, I might end up a suspect."

"Whoa. It never even occurred to me that you might be the mastermind behind the whole thing."

"I'm flattered. I'll call you later."

"Okay. Have a good day."

What was I supposed to say? No, don't call me ever again? He's dealing with a lot right now.

I wait until I hear my front door close before I bury my face in a pillow and scream.

This is bad. Not because I want to stop seeing him so no one gets hurt, but because I don't want that. I should, but I don't. I know exactly how this will play out if I let it keep going, and it's awful. But I don't want to end it.

It's selfish to keep seeing him. If only I could think of a single reason to be mad at him. Anything to justify it other than everyone else's feelings because I already know what he'd say to that reason.

But he'd be wrong. Other people do matter in this. It could never be just about us.

Thanks to not having a regular job, I'm off today. My plan was to catch up my laundry and make some new mermaid hairclips, maybe add some sequins to the new bathing suit top I bought. It's got great coverage, but it's too plain.

I can't do any of those things because they require sitting still and concentrating, and I need to get out of here, to keep moving. It just became a good day for running every errand I can come up with.

I cancel my quest for a new sports bra and push my shopping cart straight to the checkout lanes.

There's no choice. This hurts, and it's only going to get worse if I don't do something about it.

Back in my apartment, I change into pajama pants and lie on my bed, taking deep breaths. A baby gecko scurries across the outside of my closet door and then disappears into the closet through the tiny space between the door and the molding. Not a care in the world, just going wherever he wants.

I sit up and call the one person I'm willing to confide in about what I'm going through.

"I'm serious, Maren. He's wrecking my life. I just had to leave Target with only half the stuff I went for!"

"He got you kicked out of Target?"

"I had to leave because I was wearing jeans."

"That's a weird dress code for a place that sells so much denim."

"The seam in the crotch was killing me. I'm all tender and apparently, swollen, too!"

"Sounds like Malcolm killed it last night."

"Sex shouldn't hurt the next day. This is not normal."

"It might be. How many times did y'all go at it last night?"

"I don't know. A few. But no one has ever broken me like this. We're clearly not compatible."

"Clearly."

"I swear it was like he was trying to win an Olympic medal for giving a woman the most orgasms. My clit swelled more than the Grinch's heart. It should've subsided by now though, right? I've got literal big clit energy!"

"Aw, sounds like somebody learned the true meaning of Sex-mas. Did you hear a small village singing *Wel-come Ell-is come this way, fahoo fores, dahoo dores...?*"

She thinks I'm exaggerating, but I hardly am at all. And now that damn song is going to be stuck in my head for days!

"I'm in actual pain here. He's disabled me. I can't even walk around a store long enough to buy household necessities."

"Please. Your poor over-adored pussy only hurt because you were wearing tight jeans. Put on a skirt, go back to Target, and buy the rest of your stuff in comfort. Grab an ice pack while you're there so you can ice your injuries when you get home. Problem solved."

"That won't solve my Malcolm problem. I think he thinks we're dating now."

"If he's a good boyfriend, he'll be happy to come over and kiss it and make it better."

"Kiss it? He doesn't just kiss it, Maren. He *devours* it. Like a savage. I finally understand why it's called *eating* pussy. Before him, I always thought that was a stupid phrase. Because they're really just licking it, right? Uh-uh, not Malcolm. You know how some people say they lick an ice cream cone, but other people say they eat their ice cream, and that tells you *soooo* much about them as a person? Malcolm definitely eats his ice cream."

"I hardly have words to convey my sympathy for all that oral pleasure you had to endure. But thanks for that ice cream philosophy. That shit's going to keep me up at night. I think I just lick my ice cream. What does that say about me?"

"He is *not* my boyfriend."

"Fine. Tell him you only want a fuck buddy."

"I'm not telling him that! Shit, someone's at my door." I lower my voice to a whisper as I walk down the hallway. "What if it's him?"

I close my left eye, and squint through the peephole with my right. "You have got to be kidding me."

"What? Who is it?"

"Sunflowers. He fucking sent me sunflowers. Big, beautiful, bazillions of sunflowers. I can't even see the person holding them!"

"Okay, that's it. Call the cops."

I open the door and accept the flowers. "Holy shit, these are heavy."

"Yeah, tell me about it," the delivery guy says. "I didn't think you were ever going to open the door."

"Sorry. Thank you." I shut the door with my shoulder and press my back against it to be sure it closes all the way.

"He's seen my tiny apartment, Maren. Where does he think I'm going to put this giant bunch of flowers? He knows I don't have even vases for them."

"The guy's obviously an inconsiderate asshole who only thinks of himself."

"It's not even just that he's Brody's best friend. My life is so busy. The last thing I need right now is some smothering olive oil broker."

"Yeah, if only he dealt in something less suffocating, like peanut oil."

"Ha. Ha. I know his job has nothing to do with it, okay? But this isn't right."

"Who is it not right for, El? You're both adults, and you have a great time together. Stop catastrophizing and just let things happen however they happen. Will denying yourself more of his laughs and kisses and ice cream eating make you happy? Or will it make you resentful to know you've put your own wants and needs on a back burner to make other people happy? How has that worked out for you in the past?"

"Stop being rational. That's the last thing I need right now."

"Well, make up your mind. Is he the last thing you need or am I?"

She gets a laugh out of me with that.

"You know I love you and I want to support you, El, but . . ." She sighs.

"But what?"

"I think he might actually be good for you."

I gasp with an intensity that could vacuum the stink out of Baytown. "How dare you? And you call yourself my best friend."

"I'm the worst. Go find a spot for your hideous unwanted flowers, put on a skirt, and go back to Target. Love you. Mean it. Bye."

"No, Maren, wait! Come over. Please."

Maren is at my door in twenty minutes. "I had to fake a migraine to leave work early."

"You don't get migraines."

"Well, you gave me one today. Here I am. So, cure my headache, please."

"I can offer you an Oreo."

"Who in the history of the world has ever felt better after a single Oreo?"

"A whole package of Oreos?"

"Birthday cake?"

"Peanut butter."

"I'll try it. But I'm not saying for sure we won't have to have the right ones delivered."

I open my pantry and pull out a jar of rainbow sprinkles.

"You're a genius!" She takes the top off an Oreo and shakes on the sugary bits. She reassembles it, and then she pours some sprinkles in her hand and rolls the sides of the cookie through them before she takes a bite. "Okay, this is the flavor they need to release. Who do I email?"

I make myself a Maren Special Oreo, and one bite confirms she's correct. This is definitely the cookie to cure what ails us.

Someone else knocks on my door. Maren raises her eyebrows in disbelief, which I find insulting. It's one thing for me to be surprised that I have a visitor, but I don't need my best friend doubting that anyone ever comes over to hang out with me. I'm not a recluse. I just have a weird schedule.

When I look through the peephole, there's no one there. I open the door and stare down at three boxes. I quickly count twelve divided compartments. Thirty-six in all. Three dozen. Of course.

Before I even look to my left and spot him walking away, I know it was him.

Malcolm turns and walks backward for a few paces, smiles and waves. Pleased with himself, no doubt. He turns around without a word and disappears down the stairs.

I bring in the first box. "It was Malcolm."

"Damn. He brought you a whole case of wine?"

"There are two more boxes."

I bring them in, and she comes closer to check out my gift. "Those bottles are all empty."

"They're for the sunflowers."

"So, this guy, who could probably easily afford to buy you beautiful vases, brings you a bunch of empty wine bottles instead? And you're smiling about it?" She licks a sprinkle from the corner of her mouth and nods. "Yeah, go ahead and call it off. Y'all obviously don't get each other at all."

"Shut up and start putting water in these bottles."

Checking Availability
Malcolm

I LOOK AROUND THE new warehouse space I'm standing in the middle of, unsure what I'm hoping to see. Fortified walls? Armed guards? It looks just like Nico's warehouses. What the hell am I doing here?

It's only been eight days. None of the tracking numbers on the bottles have been reported yet, and they may never be, but what difference is a new warehouse going to make? All my oil is either sitting in another warehouse just like this one or being sold on unauthorized shelves at a rock-bottom discount.

And the people buying it don't have any idea it's stolen. Or they don't care. Either way, switching warehouses won't keep it from happening again.

I've known Nico for five years. No issues. Thieves find a way.

"Thanks. I'll let you know," I say to the owner of this warehouse, whose name I can't remember. I'm bad with names, but also, I don't like the guy. I liked Nico right off the bat.

I'm angry and frustrated, and worst of all, I feel helpless. And when I feel helpless, I need to do something. Anything as long as it feels productive.

It doesn't help that I had to suck it up and cancel the promo boxes this morning. And then cancel the ads. A few of the media outlets let me hold my space while everything is being redesigned.

Thankfully, one of the mills I recommended to Brody and Amanda had enough bottles of their premium olive oil to keep my first subscription box on schedule. It's not a special edition but they're having them relabeled for me so they will look special. The bottles themselves will be limited edition and the oil inside will be excellent.

None of my subscribers will ever know about the oil they almost got instead.

I'm still trying to decide if I want to rush out some last-minute promo boxes once everything is here, which is still weeks away. All the careful planning I did and paid others to do, it's all worthless now.

I grip my steering wheel and take a deep breath. New plans are coming together. All I ever promised with the subscription model was that each box would contain at least one pure extra virgin olive oil. That hasn't changed. I'm not going to let anyone down.

When I park in front of my current warehouse, Nico is there, talking to a couple of guys wearing black pants and polos. Cops? They're not in a police car, and there's no signage on the black truck next to Nico's Mercedes. Judging from their expressions, it's a serious conversation.

My gut says I should get out and make sure it's friendly.

"Hey!" Nico waves me over.

He makes the introductions. Turns out these guys are going to be installing inside cameras with infrared technology and an upgraded alarm. After looking at that other warehouse, I know Nico's security is already better than most, but I like what I'm hearing about the new stuff he's adding.

I'm not going anywhere, but I'm having the replacement bottles for the subscription boxes sent directly to the fulfillment center this time. The fewer stops and transitions, the better.

"I've got some replacement pallets coming. Probably be here at the end of the next week. Do I need to reschedule that?"

One of the security company guys shakes his head. "No, we'll be in and out of each warehouse in less than a day. We'll start with the empty ones, so there should be an upgraded space all ready for your shipment."

"Sounds good."

I shake Nico's hand and get out of the way so he can get back to business.

My head's been such a mess I haven't even tried to see Ellis since I dropped off the wine bottles. She sent me pics of all the sunflowers all over her apartment. Her smile made me smile.

It's good to have a friend in the restaurant business who will hook you up with cases of empty wine bottles on a moment's notice.

That same friend is opening a new restaurant this weekend. I've promised him I'll be there. I've also promised him some amazing olive oil as a grand opening gift. He probably expected me to do that, but I think what I've got for him is going to exceed his expectations.

Every bottle I value wasn't in that warehouse. Thank goodness.

It's Wednesday. I should probably reach out to Ellis to confirm she's available this weekend instead of just assuming she'll be my date. I'm trying really hard not to make assumptions where she's concerned.

I get her voicemail.

"Hey, I almost forgot what your voice sounded like. Sorry it's been so long. Will you let me make it up to you Saturday night? A friend of mine is opening a new restaurant, and we're on the VIP list. I come with perks. Did I mention that? Anyway, let me know if you're free. Also, are you free Friday night, too? Hell, what are you doing tonight? Call me."

She probably doesn't even listen to her messages. I send all the same information in a text. There. Now she's sure to get it.

Shit. If she doesn't listen to her messages, her inbox would've been full. It wasn't. She checks messages. And she's going to know I left a voicemail and immediately followed up with a text. Please let her see that as thorough communication and not desperation.

And please let her be available Saturday. And Friday.

And tonight.

Catching Up
Ellis

I GLANCE AT THE glass mermaid on my dresser in between folding towels. "What is he thinking? We can't go to a restaurant opening together. What if there's press? Can you imagine if a picture of us ended up online?"

She remains glassy-eyed and unconcerned about the paparazzi.

Maren would tell me to go and have a good time, to stop worrying about what might go wrong.

I have to call him and tell him something one way or the other. It's rude to leave him hanging like this.

He answers immediately. "Hello, beautiful."

"Hey, I got your messages."

"Sorry for the repetition. Just wanted to be sure you got my invitation. What are you doing right now?"

"Folding towels."

"Every time I look at one of my towels, I wish it was wrapped around you."

"Hard to believe that was almost a month ago."

"Time flies. Speaking of time, can I waste some of yours tonight?"

Why does his voice have to be so deep? It's soothing, and it makes me want to stop worrying and just be with him. I look again at the glass mermaid with her gorgeous green tail, reminding me of my big mermaid dream, and how I could never talk about it with anyone but Maren . . . until I told him.

He knows I went to mermaid camp in the Maldives, too. And he still wants to take me to a restaurant opening.

"You can come over."

"I want to take you out. I'm meeting some friends for drinks, but we don't have to stay long. We'll go to dinner after."

"Drinks with friends?" Has he lost his mind?

"Not Brody," he clarifies. "Other friends. Just a couple of restaurant owners and a wine importer. Low-key."

"Doesn't sound low-key. It sounds like I need to get dressed up."

"Saturday night we'll all be dressed up. Tonight, we're meeting at a pub, and I'd be willing to bet we'll all be in jeans. Except Tara, who might be in leggings."

"Well, if I can wear leggings."

"You can wear whatever you want. Pack an overnight bag. I want you to see my place."

"All night long?"

"All. Night. Long."

Oh, damn. That voice could melt stone, and I'm made of far weaker stuff.

"I have to work tomorrow."

"So do I. We won't be out late."

I pack a bag. No jeans. If history is any indication, that's the last thing I'll want to wear tomorrow.

Tara is indeed wearing leggings, yet still looks chic and polished, making me glad I at least bothered with jewelry and cute sandals. She owns not one, but three restaurants with a fourth in the works.

The other two friends are guys, both in jeans. One owns a single restaurant, but his second will be the one opening this weekend. He is wearing a starched white button-down shirt and cowboy boots with his jeans. I have a feeling his idea of being formally dressed would be to add a jacket, but he exudes confidence and is the kind of handsome that has probably helped open a few doors—professionally and personally.

The wine importer is the most casually dressed in a pair of worn jeans and a black t-shirt, but he speaks with a clipped accent that makes everything he says sound serious. His smile is warm and friendly, though, and his laughter comes easy.

This group of friends is so accomplished. Maren has the most traditional job of all my friends, and she's the executive assistant to a former Olympic gymnast who now owns a chain of cryotherapy facilities and two halotherapy locations, aka Himalayan salt caves—the kind people sit in to relieve ailments from asthma to eczema.

I'm not saying that stuff doesn't work, but it's not exactly mainstream medical care.

My mother's eye twitches every time Maren extols the curative benefits of either one in her presence. The fact that the cryotherapy places have nurses onsite—a necessity for the IV infusions and to do the intake evaluations for new clients before they step into the cryochambers or climb into a hyperbaric bed—and a doctor on staff for remote consultations does nothing to alleviate the twitch.

I've never introduced Mom to my friend who is a Reiki master or my craniosacral therapist. She has met the woman who made my mermaid tail, and couldn't resist telling her the potential risks of having piercings so close to her eye.

My mother would be impressed by these people I'm sitting with. Even my dad would be impressed by these people.

I listen to Malcolm talk about having to pivot to save the launch of his subscription box, thanks to the heist. That's all he says about that, but he has much more to say on the subject of olive oil.

He's hopeful about the innovations that so many Mediterranean orchards are implementing to help combat the drought conditions. He's excited to bring more awareness to South African producers, and he's especially impressed by the small-scale farmers there who are milling artisanal batches. He's eager for his next trip over. And he's intrigued by a woman in

South Texas who has consistently put out a great oil and has a new release coming soon.

When I hear him go on about the current growing conditions in various regions and the new varietals being planted, his passion is nearly infectious.

I can almost feel the romance.

Tara reminds him that her offer to host another olive oil tasting still stands. "Just let me know when you're ready. I assume I don't have to confirm this, but you can use the event to pimp your subscription box. Might not be a bad idea."

"I will definitely take you up on that soon. I'm having to get a little more creative and a lot more proactive about marketing now. Fucking thieves."

"Have they recovered any of your pallets?"

"Not so far."

They all shake their heads, and I feel myself doing the same.

"Thank God I expanded into brokerage, and I'm not solely an importer anymore. Because when you actually own the product that goes missing . . ." Malcolm exhales. "I guess I got lucky not to have been hit before now. And I've got the contacts to rebound. Focus on the positive, right?"

Emil, the wine guy says, "Let's elevate your launch party a bit. Bring over the new oil you've chosen for the first box, and I'll make sure you've got the perfect wine to pair with it."

"That was smooth," Malcolm says. "It was hardly noticeable at all how you slid right in there to market your product at my launch party." He laughs right after he says it, and then he thanks Emil.

It's obvious he knows his friend is sincerely trying to help, but they're close enough that he didn't hesitate to fuck with him for a moment before he acknowledged that.

I know Brody has friends other than Malcolm, but I never thought about Malcolm having other friends. He's traveled a lot. He owns a business supplying olive oil to restaurants and retailers alike. Why didn't I realize my brother wasn't his only friend?

There was a time when he was, but Malcolm's not that person anymore. Seeing him interacting with people I don't know, getting to know him through their reactions to him, is nice. I didn't know I would enjoy this evening so much.

He and I are not *practically family*, no matter what anyone in my actual family thinks. We were former acquaintances at best. Brody knows him well. My parents know him, though probably not as well as they think.

When I last felt like I knew Malcolm, he was so much older than me.

But I caught up. And here we are, this well-traveled, intelligent, passionate man and me, having drinks with his friends that don't include my brother.

After dinner, as we drive to his place, there isn't a single moment in the car when I want to change my mind and tell him to take me home instead.

He leads me through his sparsely decorated, but immaculate living room and down the hall to his bedroom. His condo is bigger than my apartment, more modern and freakishly clean, but his room feels cozier.

The walls are dark but the windows are tall, giving a gorgeous view of the city lights, and there's a warm glow spreading from wall sconces on either side of his bed. My eyes scan his neatly stacked pillows, two on each side, and the crisply folded-back top sheet and blanket as if housekeeping has just performed a nightly turndown service.

I wonder how often his housekeeper comes. I'm pretty sure they were here today.

"Are you judging my bed?" he asks.

"Just thinking about how I can't wait to be in it."

"Well, take your clothes off and meet me in the sheets then."

We strip like we're in a race to get naked. He wins, slides into the bed and holds the covers open for me.

"Under the covers? What a gentleman."

"I want you completely comfortable while I pleasure you for the first time in my bed."

The coverage doesn't last long. I push the blanket and sheet down far enough to watch his head move between my legs. And then he throws them off completely when my squirming unintentionally works them back up over him.

His hot mouth on my clit feels familiar now, and my body reacts to what he's doing, as well as what it anticipates he'll do next. The soft brush of his beard makes me clutch at the sheet beneath us, and my tailbone rocks upward.

My nipples swell between his thumbs and index fingers while he sucks my clit with the perfect intensity. When my back arches, his mouth never loses contact—as if he can anticipate my body's moves, too.

A sensation of warm oil flows from my memory to my core, increasing the arch in my spine and curling my toes. I fist the sheet tighter. My legs quake, and then I lose all control, gushing all over his talented tongue and his beard.

His neighbors definitely know he has company after the way I just shrieked his name.

He traces invisible shapes on my abdomen as my breathing realigns and my vision clears.

"Are you drawing hearts on my stomach like we're teenagers?" I twirl a small section of his hair and smile down at him.

"You make me feel like a teenager sometimes."

"You're a fully grown man with a successful business and a new one in the works."

"And those things rarely ever leave my mind. My brain is always spinning with worry or plans or a never-ending to do list." His fingertip scrolls a small heart just inside my hipbone, and then he plants a kiss on top of it. "Except when I'm with you."

My stomach quivers, and I can't even lie to myself and pretend it's because his beard has tickled my skin.

I don't want to think of him as a teenager, but I don't hate the thought that being with me puts the adult version of him at ease, that I might somehow provide shelter from the world for him, or at least from the hardest parts of it.

He does that for me. I feel safe with him. Emotionally safe. Free to be completely me.

"You make me feel . . ." I falter for an elegant way to say what I mean, but I know he would tell me to just say it outright, so I utter the words in the plain and simple way that I feel them. "Less afraid to fail."

His beard does tickle me now as he slides up a little, propping his elbows on either side of my body. His face hovers over my still fluttery stomach as his eyes lock onto mine. "You shouldn't fear it. No one succeeds without failing at some point."

"You don't fail."

"I've failed. They say failure is the best teacher. Of course, you've got to be willing to humble yourself enough to learn from it. That's the hard part."

"Hmm, deep."

"What they don't tell you is that spite is the best motivator. Nothing will make you want to regroup and try again like having somebody say you can't or you shouldn't or that they told you so. You already knew that, though."

"Yeah, I know all about being motivated by spite."

"Keep using it. You've got what it takes. It's just a matter of timing at this point. Sometimes, in the end, the only difference between success and failure is that the person who succeeded didn't quit. Don't quit on yourself."

"You know, if this whole olive oil thing doesn't work out, maybe you can be a life coach."

"I was thinking sex therapist."

"You are aware that doesn't mean providing therapy to someone after you have sex with them, right?"

"I refuse to be limited by other people's beliefs."

"Okay, future sex worker."

"I only wanna work for you, future mermaid." He pushes himself farther up to kiss me, but stops before our mouths meet. "I'm sorry. Current mermaid. Please forgive me, Mistress Ellisandra."

"Stop." I writhe beneath him, trying not to laugh. "Don't make things weird right now."

"You love it when I get weird."

Before I can respond, his lips land softly on mine and warmth ripples down my whole body like a gentle wave receding from the shoreline. The heat lingers after the rippling sensation fades. The kiss deepens, pulling me under, and threatening to drown every doubt I have about this, about us.

Oh, sweet Neptune. I might be falling deeply, deeply in like with this brilliant weirdo.

"Fuck me, Mal," I whisper.

"If I fuck you the way I want tonight, your legs might be too weak to swim tomorrow."

He kisses me again, and my legs are already gone.

Slippery Hopes
Malcolm

Ellis takes so long to answer her door I'm afraid she may have forgotten about the opening tonight. Or changed her mind.

The door finally opens with a flurry of apologies and flailing hand gestures.

"I'm sorry. I'm almost ready. I just need to finish my makeup. There's wine. Help yourself. I'll be right back."

Her voice is hoarse, and she won't make eye contact. She turns to walk away, but I put a hand on her shoulder. "Ellis, stop."

Her feet stop, but she doesn't turn to face me. I wrap my arms around her waist. Her whole body is tense but she lets me hold her back to my chest.

"What's wrong?"

"Nothing. I'm fine. I promise."

Loosening my grip on her waist, I say, "Look at me. Please."

Her eyes are red-rimmed and swollen. "It shouldn't have affected me like this. I'm about to start my period. I don't usually get overly emotional, but maybe my hormones are just all over the place right now."

"Slow down. What shouldn't have affected you? Let's sit and talk for a minute." She lets me lead her to the couch. "Tell me what happened."

"I've been watching the Fantasia Faeries website, waiting for the announcement about auditions. Last week, they officially announced that Shadyn, she's one of their members, was leaving the pod. This afternoon they posted that they've decided not to hold auditions at this time. What does that even mean, at this time?" She wipes her eyes with her fingers.

"I know I'm overreacting. It's not like I auditioned and found out I didn't make it, but I've been waiting so long for a chance, and I thought it was about to happen. Now, I know it's not. It may never happen. Maybe I just need to accept that I'm never going to be a part of that pod and go full-time at the spa. Do makeup on the side. I could still be an independent mermaid. It's okay to have a hobby, right?"

I hold her again, and her tears soak through my shirt. "Or maybe you should accept that this is a delay, not a denial. If you want to relegate it to a hobby, that's your choice, but it feels a little soon for that."

"Soon?" She pulls away from me. "You have no idea how long I've been working toward this!"

Okay, a little anger can be good.

"I bust my ass to keep my head above water financially so I can put my tail in the water every chance I get! And I've been doing it for nearly five years. Five long fucking years, okay? So don't tell me I'm throwing in the towel at the first setback. Because I'm not. I'm not!"

That's it. Getting pissed off leads to getting motivated.

"If I'm going to quit mermaiding, I may as well just go into banking! Maybe my dad's contact at Chase can get me a job. Guess that would take the heat off you, huh?"

Okay, we might be losing focus here . . .

"Maybe I could do niche porn, open an account where I rub olive oil over my body for money. Lube up random objects and take requests for what I should do with them. Fulfill slippery fantasies for my loyal patrons."

Turning outrage into the outrageous. I'll allow it.

"You could be my sponsor. Maybe we could cross-promote. You could put cards in all your subscription boxes with a discount code for my site."

Back the fuck up, mermaid.

"How about you go ahead and set up that site, but keep it in beta? And I'll be your first and only patron."

"I would take all your money. Leave you broke and broken hearted."

"It would be worth every penny."

She shakes her head. "You are such an enabler."

"No. I'm just your biggest fan."

"Don't make me cry again, you asshole."

"This asshole believes in you. But we're going to be late, so I need you to go dry your pretty eyes and slip a sexy dress over your beautiful body, so we can go celebrate someone else's dream tonight." I kiss the top of her head. "Your turn's coming, Ellis, and I will throw you the biggest party ever."

"And tell all your friends what, that we're partying because your girlfriend is a faerie mermaid?"

"That's exactly what I'll tell them. Proudly."

She said girlfriend. We're going to the opening, but this night has already peaked.

Ellis returns from her room and proves me wrong. Hearing her call herself my girlfriend was nice, but seeing her in this dress again is a fantasy come true.

"I thought I ruined that dress when I shoved you into the pool."

"You did. But I loved it so much, I bought it again. I had no idea when I'd get a chance to wear it, but tonight feels right."

"Tonight feels very right."

A Stripper Comes to Dinner

Ellis

I'VE SEEN MALCOLM EVERY day since the restaurant opening. Every day for two weeks, and I'm not sick of his face yet. We are officially official. Openly a couple.

In a very small circle, and the four people who I'm having dinner with tonight are outside that circle.

It feels soon to be having another family dinner at my parents' house, but Brody and Amanda have been married for two months, and our last dinner together was two weeks after the wedding, right after they got back from their honeymoon. Doesn't seem like it's been that long, but my sister-in-law posted it first thing this morning, so there's no denying it.

My sister-in-law. That's still hard to believe too. Brody's good luck is frequently unbelievable, but he really, really lucked out meeting Amanda. We all did. When I think back to some of his girlfriends before her . . . yikes.

I feel like I may have had some luck of my own recently. But my family's not ready for my lucky-in-love story yet. We'll break the news to them eventually. I have no idea how, but we'll figure it out when the time comes.

This week, I've done nothing but special effects makeup. It's been nice to be so busy, but I'm ready for some less hectic days again. My days in the spa are usually booked back-to-back, but even when my schedule is jammed there, it's still a mostly serene environment—at least in the treatment rooms. Too much of that, though, and I start to feel antsy, but too much time on movie sets and I start to crave the calm of the spa. I don't think I could ever do either one full-time.

I like when I can balance the two, but mermaiding provides a natural balance. The excitement and adrenaline of getting ready to perform creates a buzzing sensation in my veins, and then being in the water transforms the buzz to a tranquil hum. There's no way I'm ready to give that up.

I'm getting ready to head home from the set, packing up my makeup brushes and eavesdropping on a conversation I definitely should not be privy to, when Malcolm's text comes through.

> Hey, don't freak out when I walk into your parents' house. Came by your brother's place to drop off some oil Amanda wanted, and she and Brody wouldn't take no for an answer. I'm coming to dinner.

Well, damn. You never have as much time as you think.

I tell myself there's no need to overreact. It's fine. Everything will be fine. He and I have sat at my parents' table plenty of times. Not in the past eight years, but we can do this. It might even be fun.

Yeah. It's fun to have a secret.

> *Cool. I'll wear your favorite dress.*

> *That would be an act of cruelty.*

> *Kidding. I'm coming straight from work.*
> *Leggings and an oversized t-shirt. So*
> *sexxxy. Try to contain yourself.*

I look down to see how much fake blood and scar wax I've actually gotten on my shirt so I can prepare for my family's comments at dinner. Malcolm will probably join in. Hell, he'll need to if we want to keep up the charade.

It's what he would've done in the before times.

Oh, shit. This is actually his shirt—which would be fine if it was just any old shirt that happened to belong to him, but this is a Fox Olivo Imports shirt.

Honestly, wearing it on set has helped me meet a few people who might not have talked to me otherwise. The little fox on his logo is a conversation starter. I've even given these shirts to a couple of the actors, hoping they'll be photographed wearing them. Not that there are any major A-listers on this project, but exposure at any level can turn into something good.

Me wearing this shirt to dinner, however, would be significantly bad exposure.

I interrupt the production assistants who've been not-so-quietly spilling secrets in the trailer. They talk in front of me as if I'm invisible all the time. "Hey, do y'all happen to

know if there are any extra t-shirts laying around? I'm supposed
to go straight from here to my parents' house for dinner, and if
I show up with blood on my shirt, I'll never hear the end of it."

"Yeah, I know where they're at. I can grab you one, but the
image on the front might not be much better."

"Trust me. It'll be better."

I hold the requested shirt up and second-guess my claim
about it being better than the fake gore on my current shirt. Is an
irradiated stripper with neon green tears (blood?) leaking from
her eyes a bridge too far for dinner with the fam?

On any other night, I'd say yes.

Sorry little fox. You lose this round.

Brody's car isn't in the driveway. I consider circling the block a
few times so I don't have to show up first, but if I park, I can
act surprised to see Malcolm when he walks in, which somehow
seems better than having to act surprised if I'm the one walking
in to see him already here.

The only way to stop my overthinking before I get caught in
a loop is to make a choice and act on it quickly. Choice made.

I park.

My mom's eyes go straight to my shirt. "Really, Ellis?"

"Sorry. It's the film I've been working on. The shirt I was wearing all day was covered in fake blood and wax. It was disgusting."

"And you thought that would be a better option?"

"Trust me. It's better. But I'm happy to change if you're offering an alternative."

"Come with me."

I follow her all the way into her closet. She presents me with a hot pink scrubs top that has smiley faces all over it.

"You can't be serious."

"Scrubs are comfortable. They'd actually be perfect for when you're doing special effects makeup. They're made to be covered in blood."

"Do you not have an old t-shirt I can borrow? What about Dad?"

She huffs, but she digs through his t-shirt drawer. "Here."

I unfold the shirt. "I am not wearing this."

"You asked for a t-shirt."

"Not this one." The shirt references a hurricane from the eighties. The shirt is also from the eighties. It says *Alicia was a Bitch!*

"Your father got sent home from school for wearing that. It's one of his favorite stories."

"We've all heard it a million times. I know he loves this ratty old shirt, but does he have anything less ancient I can borrow? I'd hate to be the reason this one finally fell apart."

"Oh, we're being picky. Do you have a date after you leave here?"

"No, but I don't have to have a date to care about my appearance."

Again, she eyes my current shirt. "Right."

She gives me a second option from Dad's shirts. More meteorological humor:

What's the difference between weather and climate?

You can't weather a tree, but you can climate.

His humor has toned down significantly over the years, yet somehow, not matured at all. At least this one's not threadbare.

I manage to act appropriately shocked and barely happy to see Malcolm with Brody and Amanda. Brody takes one look at my shirt and says, "Did you have a wardrobe malfunction?"

"Almost."

And we almost make it through dinner before dad feels the need to share doomsday predictions about the future of olive oil, given the drought situation, which he can promise us all isn't going to end any time soon.

Malcolm counters by very calmly and rationally sharing the methods growers are using to tackle the problem, from altered irrigation techniques to the drought-resistant species of olives that are being planted. Dad's response is basically, "too little, too late" to everything Malcolm says.

I grip my fork and grit my teeth through as much of it as I can stand before I say, "Do you have to be such a pessimist, Dad? Would you prefer people did nothing?"

"No, I'd prefer the world had listened about climate change before we got to this point."

"Well, we're here, and isn't it better if they listen now than not at all?"

"I agree," Brody says. "Maybe we can't turn around everything that's been set in motion, but some of the greatest innovations have come out of some of the worst times."

"Necessity is the mother of invention," Amanda adds.

"I'm just suggesting it might be time for Malcolm to diversify. That's all."

I want to shout that he is diversifying. He's just not abandoning olive oil. He can't. That would be giving up on his passion. No one should be told to do that. I've lost my appetite.

Malcolm takes my dad's criticism in stride, but he sticks to his guns. "I don't think it's time to throw in the towel just yet. But I'm watching what's happening around the world. Watching and listening."

Dad can't let it go. "You better be. What are you thinking for the future?"

"I'm thinking olive oil will find a way."

Damn, he doesn't get upset, but it doesn't seem like he's going to let my dad have the last word either. And if there's one thing Gary French hates, it's not getting the last word.

"Real estate might be the way."

Without missing a beat, Malcolm says, "I'm not sure I'm ready to start my own orchard, but I'm not ruling it out for the future."

We all laugh, even mom. Dad doesn't laugh exactly, but he does shift his focus. To me.

"I assume you're still cobbling together a livable wage doing facials and creating realistic bullet wounds on actors?"

"And mermaiding. I'm performing next month in Miami."

Malcolm's brows lift. "That sounds interesting."

"It's a hotel opening. If you're going to be a mermaid at a hotel opening, it's probably going to be in Miami."

I can tell he's shocked that I haven't mentioned it.

"Will you be performing all weekend?" Amanda asks. "Or is it a single show? How does that work?"

"There are a few choreographed performances, but honestly, we'll spend more time lying on the island in the middle of the pool, jumping in and showing off for the guests. The pool has a viewing wall so people can see us as we swim by or stop to blow bubble kisses. It should be a fun gig."

"That's so cool!" Amanda's enthusiasm goes a long way toward making my dad's disgruntled expression easier to ignore. "I wish I had vacation days left. I'd love to come see you perform."

"Swim," Dad says. "She swims."

"While performing," I say. "But getting paid to swim isn't unheard of. It's an actual sport. At the top levels, they earn prize money and sponsorships—"

"Oh, I'm sorry," he says. "I guess I missed the announcement about Houston's pro mermaid team. How much do you aquatic athletes get paid at your level?"

"I'm getting three grand for the weekend at the hotel opening. Plus travel expenses."

"That ridiculous."

"Well, make up your mind, Dad." I pull my napkin from my lap and toss it onto the table. "Do I not make enough money or do I make too much?"

I push my chair back, stand, and walk away to clear my plate.

Staring at myself in the mirror over my parents' dresser, I wish I was unbothered when my dad scoffed at mermaiding, a wish for armor that his words can't penetrate. My arms shake as I remove his stupid shirt, fold it, and leave it on the bench at the end of their bed.

When I walk back into the dining room to say my goodbyes, all eyes go to the deteriorating stripper hanging off my tits.

Brody chokes on his iced tea. "That's an even more interesting shirt choice."

"Haven't you heard, big brother? That's what I do. I keep things interesting in this family."

He smiles and nods—his way of saying he's proud of me for staying calm. Sibling communication is subtle sometimes. There was a time when my dad and I would've been in a full-blown argument at this point. But tonight, I'm simply leaving.

Malcolm stands. "I'll walk you out."

My eyes flash a warning. That is not what he would've done before.

"I really need to get going, too," he says. "Thank you so much for dinner, Nora. He hugs Mom in her chair and then extends a hand to my father, who looks up at him suspiciously, but completes the handshake.

Malcolm nods at Brody and Amanda before we leave them to the wolves.

I power walk to my car at the curb. "Are you proud of me?" I ask.

"Why didn't you tell me?"

"About the mermaid gig? It's just a one-time thing."

"As a mermaid. You talk to me about your other jobs, but you never mentioned this."

"I just got the offer a few days ago."

"That must've felt good after the recent let down about the auditions. Why didn't you share it with me?"

"You've been busy. You have a lot going on."

"There was time."

"I just didn't think it was a big deal."

"It's the biggest deal. It's the thing that matters most to you. And when important things happen in your life, good or bad, I want to know about them. They're important to me, too."

"This is so unfair."

"What? That I care about you?"

"No, that I want to hug you right now, but I can't."

He steps forward, but I back up. "No. Don't. Not here."

"Your place or mine?"

"Mine. I don't have a bag packed."

"I'll see you there. And you can tell me all about this mermaid job like you just found out about it."

"We're into role playing now?"

"We might be. Or this might be a good night for your first spanking."

"I like you when you're dirty."

"That would be all the time."

"Draw your own conclusions. See you at my place."

Seeing Signs
Malcolm

I FOLLOW HER INSIDE and shake my head at the hot glue gun on her kitchen island. I'm a neat freak, but her place always has some small thing out of place, something she didn't get around to putting away after she used it, or a protein bar wrapper on the coffee table, maybe a stray sock that fell out of a laundry basket in the middle of the hallway.

Those types of things used to make me crazy, but in her apartment, they make me smile. Little signs of her.

"You can't imagine how hard it was not to stand up for you when your dad treated you like that."

Ellis drops her purse on top of the hot glue gun as if it's invisible. "Thank you for not doing that. And even if we end up telling them that we're seeing each other at some point, still please don't do that, okay? I have to handle him myself."

"*If* we end up telling them at some point?"

"I meant when, but I can't think about that without my stomach clenching, so *if* came out instead. Just so you know, I wanted to take up for you, too."

"Are you sucking up to me to try to get out of having your pretty little ass spanked?"

"We should talk."

She takes a deep breath, and my heart stutters because that is the absolute worst opening to a conversation. Bottled sunflowers hang their heads on every flat surface from her kitchen counters to her coffee table. As if they're praying for me. Or they have their necks snapped.

"Okay," I say. "I'm listening."

"The role-play thing? Not really into it. Punishment play? Hard no."

"So, you just like a little pain for the escapism."

"No, it's the opposite of that, I think. I don't know how to explain it, but I want to be present, not to escape it."

"But focusing on being spanked makes everything else fall away for you."

"Yeah."

"Do you always like it or only sometimes?"

"I'd definitely let you know if I didn't want you to do it."

"Because it's easier for you to say what you don't want than what you do."

"That's everybody, right?" She bites her bottom lip.

"Some people have an easier time asking for what they want than others."

"I guess I just want the person I'm with—"

"To be able to read your mind."

She laughs. "Guilty."

"No judgment. I don't think I'll ever be able to read your mind, but I'm pretty sure I can learn to read your body." I step close enough to brush her hair off her cheek.

"Do you have any deviant kinks I should know about?" She asks the question tentatively, like she's not sure she really wants to know.

"Okay, first of all, I don't think of spanking as deviant. But no, none that I'm aware of. Of course, my gauge for deviancy might not be the same as yours."

"Well, on that note, let's go to bed."

Kissing her in her kitchen feels like we've always been intimate, like knowing her before when she was so young and I was so immature is just a false memory.

"I have one more question," I say, making intense eye contact as if I might be about to ask something pivotal. To be fair, she deserves the suspense after the threat of *we should talk*.

"I'm listening."

"How long are you going to keep these dead sunflowers all over your apartment?"

Her shrug is quick, her smirk playful. "Until you replace them, I guess."

I've held her wrists against the mattress, dug my fingers into her hips when she's on top, squeezed and caressed just about every inch of her . . . having any part of her body in my hands feels amazing. But watching my hand land on her sexy ass is so fucking incredible.

Knowing she's enjoying it is intoxicating. I rub over the redness, noticing the heat I've caused there. The way her body melts a little more each time I soothe the sting makes me want to hide away from the world with her for a long, long time. Not escapism, but a true escape.

We need a vacation. I need to take her somewhere far, far away where we don't know anyone, so there'll be no need to worry about anyone seeing us together.

Soon.

Right now, I need to feel her tight pussy drenching my fingers, my beard, and eventually, my dick.

Tonight, I'll fuck her like she belongs to me.

Tomorrow, I'll replace her flowers.

And someday soon, we'll escape.

Checking Lists
Ellis

MY SHOPPING CART ROLLS a few feet away from me while I dig through boxes of tea bags, hoping to find a hidden package of my favorite at the back of the shelf. I glance over my shoulder to see who moved it, annoyed because I don't see how it could've been in anyone's way.

"Who are you shopping for?" Brody asks, surveying the contents of my cart he's commandeered.

I yank it back from him. "Y'all grocery shop together? That is so codependent."

"I'm short," Amanda says. "When I bring him, I don't have to ask strangers to get things from the top shelves for me."

"Oh, please. You're gorgeous. I'm sure strange men looooove helping you."

My brother rolls his eyes. "That's cute. But seriously, who the hell are you shopping for? You hate these cheese and peanut butter crackers. And since when do you eat summer sausage?" He rummages through my basket like it's a bargain bin. "Barbecue flavor pork rinds? Okay, what's his name?"

"What? Who? Nobody." I slap at his hands. "Get out of my snacks."

"These are not your snacks. You snack on things you can dip in hummus or ranch dressing. And cookies." He stares at the pork rinds for a moment before dropping them back into my basket. "The only person I know who eats those things is Malcolm."

"Pretty sure if he was the only person who ate them, factories would stop making them."

Why is it so hot in here? Is this aisle getting narrower?

"Must be serious if you're buying him snacks to keep at your place. Why is he a secret?"

"I don't have a secret boyfriend, okay? Mind your own business."

"Why are you getting so mad?"

"I'm just trying to buy groceries!"

He holds up his hands. "And I'm just wondering who you're buying them for. Why are you so agitated? Please tell me he's not married."

I white-knuckle the handle of my cart. "Don't make me slam this thing into you because I will crack your ribs like crab legs."

Amanda puts her hand on Brody's arm. "Whoa. Both of you need to calm down. Your sister doesn't have to tell you every detail of her life. But he was just teasing you about the snacks, Ellis. Your reaction was pretty extreme."

"She's obviously keeping a secret," Brody says. "I just want to make sure she's not doing anything stupid."

"Why? Because you think I can't make smart decisions? Do you honestly think I'd be dating a married man?"

"I don't know what to think based on the way you're freaking out. But I know you don't eat any of this shit." He gestures over my cart.

I back my cart up and angle it to go around him. "You have no idea what I eat."

He jumps in front of my cart, grabs the pork rinds again, and tosses them at me. "Fine. Here. Prove it."

Amanda shakes her head. "Brody, stop. She doesn't have to prove anything."

I glare at my brother as I rip into the bag.

Neptune below, do they always smell like this?

Holding my breath, I pull out what must be the biggest pork rind in the package and aggressively crunch into it until the whole thing has been reduced to sawdust in my mouth.

"Mmmmmm, delithious!" A spray of crumbs leaves my mouth as I declare my love for these salty crimes against my tastebuds.

Brody reaches into the bag and takes a couple of pork rinds for himself, shaking his head as he walks off, unknowingly eating a snack meant for his best friend.

Part of me wants to tell him right here and now just to watch him choke on it. But we've caused enough of a scene. Amanda is standing still, staring at me like she thinks we've both lost our minds.

Welcome to the family!

I smile at her apologetically, pull a hair clip out of my purse to close the bag, and cut my shopping trip short to avoid running into my brother again.

If I told him that I keep a toothbrush and a spare menstrual cup in Malcolm's bathroom now, he'd choke for sure.

Does he suspect? Is that why he mentioned Malcolm's name? No, now I'm just being ridiculous.

I'm not even sure why I picked today to start stocking my kitchen with Malcolm's favorite snacks. I leave tomorrow for the hotel opening in Florida. Maybe it was thinking about how much I'm going to miss him that made me do it.

We're getting too comfortable. Too careless. Then again, it's not like I expected to run into Brody and Amanda in the grocery store.

I should move to another part of town.

Right. Like I can afford to move anywhere. Since the horror flick wrapped, I haven't had any new makeup jobs, not even a photo shoot or a wedding. The spa is part-time at my request, and my bank balance is currently making me rethink that decision.

But every time I get worried and think maybe I need to go on the books full-time, something always comes through.

Like this weekend in Miami. Perfect timing.

I dump the pork rinds into a resealable storage bag to keep them fresh. If someone had told me a few months ago that I'd have these things in my pantry . . . well, the only prediction that would've shocked me more is being told that I'd be sucking Malcolm Fox's dick on a regular basis.

But here I am, storing special snacks just for him while staring down a weekend in Miami at a luxury hotel and wishing he was going with me.

I know he can't get away right now, but that didn't stop me from wanting to ask him anyway.

With the groceries all put away, I doublecheck my packing list. I make lists now. Physical lists, not just in my head. I call it the Malcolm Effect.

I kick a discarded sports bra under my bed in defiance of his influence, and then I laugh, knowing that if he sees it, he's going to pick it up and put it in my hamper. Last week, I watched him tidy up my kitchen as if I wasn't there.

He'd gone to get himself a beer from my fridge, but on the way back to the living room, he straightened a stack of mail on the end of my counter, threw an empty sparkling water can in the recycling bin, and relocated a bowl and spoon from the sink to the dishwasher.

When I'm at his place, I rearrange the throw pillows on his couch. They always look so stiffly placed, so I lift each one and toss it back randomly, letting it lay where it lands. It gives them a casual slouch, makes the whole couch look more inviting. I know as soon as I leave, he straightens them again, but I'm going to keep doing it. They're literally called *throw* pillows.

All the items on my bedroom list are in my suitcase already. My tail is zipped into its carrying bag and hanging from a hook on my door. There's a separate list on my bathroom counter so I don't forget anything from there and a checklist on my front door just to be sure I don't arrive at the airport to realize I've forgotten my ID or phone charger.

This part of me may be new, but I've always had more than one side. This weekend, I'm Ellisandra, the mermaid who's going to wow the crowd and enjoy every damn minute of it.

And thanks to her boyfriend's influence, there is no chance she'll forget her tail or her waterproof eyeshadow.

Going Big
Ellis

SEDONA RAIN TAKES ROLL, makes sure all six of her hired mermaids are present and in their tails. I've worked for her several times since the camp in the Maldives, but it's been a while. She nods at my new tail. "This is beautiful."

"Thanks. I'm pretty proud of it."

"Make me proud in that pool."

"You got it."

We are all being carried out on shell-shaped beds by tanned, oiled-up cabana boys. Their oiled bodies take my mind back to a scene I don't have time to reminisce right now.

I have to be fully Ellisandra right now, in the moment and focused on my moves and my safety.

With a pair of oily-muscled carriers positioned by each of us, Sedona smiles and asks the question she always asks before her mermaids dive in. "What is the most important thing you have to do out there?"

We all answer in unison: "Live to swim another day!"

"Exactly. My eyes aren't the only ones that will be watching to be sure you're safe, but it's ultimately up to you to listen to your own body. This isn't a cold-water tank, but that doesn't ensure you won't get a cramp. It's going to be a long day. If you need assistance at any point, give the sign. One of the guys will jump in and steal you from the pool. It will be just another part of the show as far as anyone knows. We'll get you safely back on the island. Don't panic, but don't be stupid either. Stay hydrated. There is shade. Use it."

She pauses, waits for us all to acknowledge our understanding.

"We've got dense foliage arranged in the center of the island to create an enclosed space that we will be referring to as The Jungle. If you need to reapply sunscreen, readjust, or do anything that would break the illusion of being a magical mermaid, you signal one of the guys. He will drag you into The Jungle. Stolen mermaids can be a part of the show at any time."

Again, we all nod to let her know we've heard and understood.

"Do not, under any circumstances, swim into the grotto to tug on your tail or reposition your shells. There will be VIPs hanging out in the grotto. You are encouraged to swim through and entertain them, but this is a family event. If anyone is inappropriate, you let one of us know as discreetly as possible. It will be taken care of. There will be guests in the pool, but you're going to stay between the island and the viewing wall. There's plenty of pool space that keeps you in our sight. Be smart. Be safe. Be what you came here to be, which is . . ."

Six voices respond: "Magical Mermaids!"

"Gentlemen, let's present our mermaids."

One by one, we are carried out to the pool area and paraded around the perimeter to the footbridge that leads to the island.

People whistle and cheer. Children scream and jump up and down when they see us. I love this part, but I cannot wait to be in the pool, doing barrel rolls and flips and spins, blowing bubble kisses at wide-eyed kids.

Our beds are lowered to the island close to the water's edge. The sides slope so we can easily roll into the pool. Once we're all in the water, our beds are pulled back into the shade, ready for our return.

We spread out and pair off to perform a brief choreographed routine that allows us to break the surface dramatically for air twice, and ends with tail high-fives between each pair. When we split apart after, we all play to the crowd, undulating like dolphins so they can see how our tails propel us, and then slowing down to make elegant ascensions back to the surface.

I blink water from my eyes until I spot an excited group of kids gathered in front of the wall and dive back down to blow my first round of bubble kisses.

Another mermaid swims over to entertain them, and I swim off to let her have the spotlight. This will be a repeat performance throughout the day. In between, we will be lifted back onto the island and carried to our beds.

We will take staggered extended lunch breaks in pairs, and then we will all leave the area for several hours in the late afternoon, returning for an evening performance. It's going to be a pain to leave the pool for so long, and then have to get ready again, but tomorrow is a much shorter day.

If I get tired today, I'll find some more excited kids to entertain, and think of that three grand hitting my bank account. I can finally pay off my tail.

This is what I train for, and this pool is beautiful.

The photographer enters the pool to get underwater shots of each of us.

A gig like this makes me think maybe it's no big deal if I never get to audition for the Fantasia Faeries. But the reality is that opportunities like this are few and far between on your own.

I know three of the mermaids here today, but I've never met the other two. Networking is important, and I'm super grateful to be here with these talented women. One of the new mermaids is my partner in our group performances. She tells me at lunch that she knows another promoter who runs things very much the way Sedona does, and offers to tell her about me.

Good things happen after chance encounters sometimes.

When we reenter the pool for the afternoon, I spend some time on the island, preening for the crowd, and then pretending to be captured by one of the cabana boys and dragged into The Jungle. He and I hide out for a bit, laughing about the absurdity of it before I make my escape and roll out to wave to the crowd.

After my return has been sufficiently celebrated, I slide back into the pool and swim to the wall to see who's watching and waiting for a new mermaid to entertain them.

No way. He's here? He's really here?

Malcolm smiles, walks to the glass, and taps his fingers in a wave. If I hadn't just had a long break, I'd be afraid I was hallucinating. He flew to Miami for this?

I tap my fingertips against his, push back from the glass, and blow air between my fingertips, dragging the bubbles up, around, and down to seal the heart.

His eyes widen along with his smile. He's impressed.

So am I.

When I surface again, I can't swim over to talk to him because when I'm in the pool, I'm a mermaid. And mermaids don't talk to impetuous guys who've flown over 900 miles to see them. But they can smile and wave.

And back underwater, they can perform just for him. No one ever has to know. Mermaids are very good at keeping secrets.

His eyes follow me every time I swim near him. The ending of the show involves each of us being stolen, pulled back to the island, and ultimately dragged into The Jungle, where we can rest for a few minutes before we're carried back to our beds, back over the foot bridge, and paraded back into our dressing room in the hotel.

Thankfully, we're allowed to wave at and talk to the crowd as we leave. Unfortunately, I'm not done for the day. There's still the evening portion to perform.

Once I'm out of my tail and wrapped in a towel, I text Malcolm to let him know the details of my schedule. I'm not able to invite him in because we all share the same dressing area. I'm still a magical mermaid until ten o'clock, whether I'm in the pool or not.

I was looking forward to this three-hour break, but now it feels excruciating. We're not supposed to go back to our rooms because mermaids don't take elevators. And they can't exhaust themselves with secret sex before they have to perform again. They have to live to swim another day.

He says he understands. No worries. He'll be here when I'm done.

Twenty minutes before I'm due to be carried back out for the evening performance, he texts again.

> Hope you've had a good day. Mine's been amazing. I saw the most beautiful mermaid in the world. She blew me kisses. And I'm about to see her again. How lucky am I?

It's a good damn thing all my makeup is waterproof. I used to hate cheesy shit like this.

He's turning me into one of those women who swoons for grand gestures. I'd tell myself I'm not falling for it—if he hadn't already captured me.

Maren is the only person close to me who has ever seen me perform. No one else has cared enough to bother.

He made the time, in spite of everything he has going on right now. He fucking bothered. In a big way.

The night session flies by, but knowing Malcolm is waiting for me makes the necessary prep for tomorrow seem to take forever. All our mermaid regalia is hanging from racks around the dressing area. The hotel has provided all the right mats, fans, and plenty of towels. Tails have been cleaned and finally, I can head upstairs to clean myself.

But first, I need to give Malcolm the biggest hug.

My hair is twisted up under a ball cap and I'm wearing baggy sweats and an oversized t-shirt. We have to be as un-mermaid-like as possible as we move through the hotel between shows. It's not impossible that someone could recognize us, but the less attention we draw when we're tail-less, the better.

He recognizes me immediately, and his whole face lights up.

"Thanks for hanging around. I know it's late."

"Of course. Are you hungry? Do you want a drink?"

"All I need is a shower. But if you're hungry, please feel free to grab something while I'm scrubbing the sunscreen and chlorine off my body and out of my hair."

"How about I get us a bottle of wine and some snacks? Text me your room number and I'll meet you there in half an hour?"

"Yes, please."

Fresh from the shower, I scroll through the hotel's social media to see if any pictures are up yet from today's performances. The photographer has already posted a few shots, but not the underwater images. He'll edit those because they're going on the hotel's website, and they're technically part of our compensation package.

Professional shots are expensive. It's always nice when an event has an official photographer and we're offered images for our own portfolios.

There are comments from guests, all glowing so far. People are mostly talking about how stunning the hotel is, but a few have mentioned the mermaids.

All positive press.

Malcolm arrives with the wine and two magnificent slices of chocolate cake. He is such a keeper.

He pours the wine, and I remind him to go easy on mine. I have to be up early and ready to swim tomorrow.

"Easy on the sugar, too? Should we share a slice?"

"When have you ever seen me willingly share cake?"

We sit on the bed and devour our slices, sipping the wine and talking. He tells me over and over again how great I was today. He's the hype man every mermaid needs.

"I still can't believe you're here." I steal the last bite of strawberry from the top of his cake.

"I'm just grateful you're not mad."

"Why would I be mad?"

"I wasn't sure how you'd feel about me inserting myself into this part of your life with no warning."

"Yet, you showed up anyway."

"Sometimes the possibility of having to ask for forgiveness is less scary than the thought of asking permission."

"Ah, I should've known you were a forgiveness over permission guy."

"Not in most areas. But I didn't want to risk you telling me not to come. So, yeah, I showed up not knowing how you'd feel about it. Sometimes, you just have to take a chance."

"I feel flattered that you went to the trouble. And happy."

"Good because I'm really happy I got to see you in your element, doing your thing. It was cool."

"I liked hearing you talk about your job with your friends. That felt like seeing you in your element."

"You'll get to see the full show at the launch party. Oh, I forgot to tell you, they recovered twenty pallets of my stolen oil."

"That's great. Maybe they'll find the rest, too."

"I'm not holding my breath, but it's nice to get some of it back."

"Tomorrow's a shorter day. Maybe we can do something in the evening after I'm done. If you have time before your flight."

"I'm here until Monday. We're on the same flight home."

"How'd you manage that?"

"It wasn't hard to figure out once you told me what airline you were on and what time you'd land in Houston. I bought my ticket not long after you bought yours."

"I'm not sure if it's worrisome that you pay such close attention or impressive."

"Be impressed. You get scary when you're suspicious."

"I'm always scary."

"You're terrifying, Buttercup." He wipes chocolate from my mouth with his thumb.

"Don't you forget it." I finish the wine in my glass and decline a second. "Can I ask about your family? You never talk about them, and growing up, I never really knew what the deal was, just that you were at our house a lot."

"You can ask me anything. My parents took turns disappearing when I was growing up, and my grandmother was more of a parent than either one of them even when they were around. Mom and I lived with her mom off and on, until we ultimately lived there permanently. My dad's parents saw me when I was little, but after he took off for the final time when I was fourteen, I didn't see them anymore. Haven't seen him or his parents since."

"Do you still see your grandmother who raised you?"

"She died a few years ago. But Mom's still in Houston. She's grown up considerably, doesn't disappear anymore, has a steady job, but she is who she is. Let's just say I don't agree with all her choices."

"At least she's stable now."

"More stable than she was when I was a kid, but I pay her rent. She mostly manages to keep up with her car note and utilities."

"Oh. That must be hard."

"I've learned to accept that she does the best she can. I love my mom, but I can't live with her, and I can't let her not have a safe place to live, so I cosigned the lease, and I pay for it."

"Your dad has never grown up enough to attempt an adult relationship with you?"

"Couldn't even tell you where he lives. Or if he's alive, for that matter."

"Wow. So, my dad was the only one you had."

"Still is."

"He's not always the best."

"He's a lot better than mine ever bothered to be. And he means well. Communication's not his best skill."

"Unless he's communicating about hurricanes."

"Even then, he's a behind-the-scenes guy, not the guy you put in front of the camera."

I laugh at the accuracy. "You are so right. Can you even imagine my dad as a TV weatherman? He lacks charisma."

"He has his own brand of charm."

"A little bit of it goes a long way."

"Yeah, but he'd fight a hurricane for you or Brody."

"I know. He loves you, too."

"I know."

We recork the wine and watch TV until I'm falling asleep on his shoulder.

He kisses me goodnight at the door to my room like we're ending a date. I definitely make it clear he can stay, but he says he doesn't want to be the reason my legs are too weak to perform tomorrow.

Flattering himself in his favorite way, but I'm tired and I do need sleep, so I let him leave.

I'm glad he didn't ask me if I wanted him to come here for the hotel opening. I might've said no, been afraid that I'd be more anxious with him here. Nothing would've been further from the truth.

Playing to the Crowd
Malcolm

EMIL HAD ALL THE wine delivered to Tara's latest restaurant this morning for my launch party. I actually had another venue booked, but the more I thought about hosting a tasting to coincide with marketing the subscription box, the more it made sense to do that as part of the launch instead.

My initial guest list for the tasting had fifty names. I gave five friends who are chefs five invitations each. That netted twenty-five wealthy Houstonians with their plus-ones. And I invited my own people to include Brody and Amanda, some of my retail clients, Ellis, of course, her best friend Maren and her date.

Maren said a few of the doctors she knows from her job might be interested as well as the owner, so I sent out a second round of invites to add them.

We've got seventy-five seats, which is a hell of a big tasting, but Tara's staff is well-versed in the oils and the wines we're pairing them with, so we're as ready as we're ever going to be.

This is a seafood restaurant, and I have a special surprise for Ellis. While I was waiting for her after her last performance in Miami, I got to know the event photographer. He showed me all the underwater shots he'd taken of her, and one of them was so damn breathtaking, I knew I had to have a copy.

And I still needed to get Tara a thank you gift for hosting my event. She's got an upscale vintage sea theme in the décor here. I saw immediately that a large gilt-framed print of my favorite mermaid would look spectacular on the wall outside the private dining room.

The photographer edited it to look like an old painting, and you'd never know the picture was taken in a pool and not the ocean. It's a perfect fit for this place.

Ellisandra's image is the first thing you see when you enter the dimly lit hallway, and she's undeniably eye-catching, beckoning you to come closer in the glow of the picture light hanging above the frame.

The waitstaff say they love having her there because *follow the mermaid* is the best way ever to give directions.

She has no idea she's hanging on the wall here in all her mermaid glory. I can't wait to see her face when she sees herself lit up like a masterpiece.

People are arriving, and when I hear "follow the mermaid" for the first time, it sounds like excellent advice.

Ellis walks in just ahead of Brody and Amanda, along with Maren and her date, which means I am limited to greeting them as a group, but unable to greet her the way I want.

I think the statute of limitations is running out on our secret. I'm ready to face the consequences. Not tonight, of course.

My friends have all been briefed on the situation, and I've taken shit from each of them about having to be a secret boyfriend. They're all right, of course. It's ridiculous, but it's how we began, so coming out as a couple now is going to be a whole thing.

I get pulled away to answer some last-minute questions about the party that will follow the tasting. The restaurant is closed for my event, and we are expecting upwards of two hundred people to attend the second half.

I'm nervous, but excited, a condition Ellis calls nervecited. That sums it up well.

The staff is getting everyone seated for the tasting. Emil and I will enter the room after they've all taken their places. He's going to give a short introduction to the wines, but it's not a truly joint promotion. My subscription box is the main feature. But Emil is knowledgeable about olive oil, too, so having him participate in this is the best possible scenario.

I'm fine with a little wine promo happening. It's an add-value for the attendees, and it keeps the tasting from feeling too much like a sales pitch.

When I step into the hallway, Brody is exiting the bathroom. We walk toward the private dining room together. He stops at the mermaid and stares.

"Is that . . . that's my sister."

"Yeah. Tara needed something for that space, and I knew Ellis was a mermaid. Seemed like a good fit."

"So, you just reached out to her and asked for this picture? How'd you know she'd have something like this? I've never seen it before."

"I wasn't sure what kind of pictures she'd have, but I figured it was worth a shot. And this one was perfect."

"It looks great. Just sort of weird to be seeing her like this."

"We should get inside," I say, adjusting my tie. Was it crooked? I have no idea. Is it choking me all of a sudden? So much.

"People are engaged in the tasting, genuinely showing interest in the oils. I wasn't sure what to expect. Some people will come to these types of things just because a friend of theirs is coming, but I think we got the right group of attendees."

When the subscription cards are collected, Tara gives me a quick smile and nod that tells me they're not all blank. There will be more cards available during the party, and I will give a condensed version of the spiel I gave in here to entice more people to subscribe.

The oils are all featured in the tapas that will be served throughout the rest of the night and there are small signs on every table, describing each selection.

My nerves are still zinging a little, but having the VIP tasting out of the way helps. I don't mind having eyes on me for a presentation, but I'm ready to mingle. And more than ready to steal a few moments alone with Ellis on the back patio.

As we exit the private dining room, I hear Brody ask her, "When did you pose for that painting?"

For fucks sake. Way to confuse her, Brody.

I look at her face so I don't miss her surprise, but I know I'm going to need to intervene and steer the conversation until she picks up that her brother thinks she already knew about it. Damn. This just got sticky.

She stares in disbelief for a moment. "I don't know," she says, shaking her head as if she doesn't recognize it.

"It's the photo you and I talked about." I try not to put too much obvious emphasis on anything. "When I reached out to the photographer after you gave me his information, I explained the vintage feel of the décor, and he offered to edit the shot to fit the vibe."

Her expression makes it abundantly clear she still doesn't have a fucking clue what I'm talking about. Shit. She can't go along if she can't even catch on. I've got to give her more.

"I know you probably didn't expect it to be that big, but as soon Tara saw it, she said she knew exactly where and how she wanted to hang it." I wave my hand at the frame and continue talking way too fast. "And, so here you are, all edited and spot-lighted. Can you believe it?"

"No. I really can't." Her expression shifts. Not in the way I had hoped. She steps past me and heads for the bathroom.

Brody shrugs, laughs, and says, "She was in a good mood earlier. Guess it's not her favorite picture of herself." He walks off toward the main dining room.

Amanda lingers with me at the end of the hall for a moment, studying my face in a way that makes me want to cover it. She's too perceptive for her own good, and way too intuitive for my comfort right now. "She looks so beautiful as a mermaid."

"She's always beautiful."

She smiles, and I know in an instant I've given away too much.

Maren shoots me a look that says I'm the biggest dumbass in town as soon as I walk into the party already in swing. I took a break in Tara's office to regroup, but it wasn't long enough.

I need to find Ellis and get her alone to explain. She seemed angry, and that was the last thing I expected. Why would she be mad? Because Brody knew about it before she did? I can explain that. I can explain everything.

Emil has the microphone, and he's calling me forward to speak. It's time to recite the spiel for the subscription box again. I can do this in my sleep, but it will land better if I show slightly more awareness. *Focus, dammit.*

The words leave my mouth on auto-pilot. My eyes scan the crowd the entire time. I can't find her. She must've stepped outside. That's good. Outside is good.

As soon as I hand the mic back to Emil, I make my way through the crowd, heading for the doors to the patio. Once I've pushed through them, I can finally take a full breath. No one is out here.

"Ellis?" No answer.

I slip back inside, but I skirt the crowd this time, making my way to the front entrance.

She's not out front either. Did she go back into the bathroom? That has to be it.

Leaning on the wall outside the women's restroom, I decide I'll give her two more minutes before I go in. Tara walks by and saves me.

"Can you see if Ellis is in there, please? I need to tell her something."

"Sure."

I peak inside when she opens the door, but I don't see Ellis's hair or my favorite green dress.

Tara comes out and says she's not in there.

Back in the main dining room, I search for Maren. She's gone, too.

Fuuuuck!

I can't leave. I can't go after her, can't call her . . . I have to put on a happy face and mingle. This event is too important for me to blow. After news of the heist broke, I fielded phone calls for days, ensuring people I hadn't suffered any great losses and their orders wouldn't be interrupted. I know how to rally in a crisis. I've got this.

But I'm going straight to her place when I leave here.

Until then, I'll mingle and answer questions with a smile on my face. A big, fat, fake fucking smile.

Off Script

Ellis

MAREN TRIED TO GIVE Malcolm the benefit of the doubt from every possible angle on the drive home.

He sees you as a literal work of art, babe.

I really think he just finds you so beautiful and fascinating . . .

It was a shock, sure, and yeah, he could've warned you, but maybe just hear him out?

Every attempt only heightened my anger. Her poor date. He thought he was going to have a great night at a party where he could network and spread the good word about cryotherapy.

Well, dude, I guess none of us got the night we'd bargained for, did we?

I've gone from pacing in my kitchen while devouring a handful of Oreos to absently pulling loose threads from the blanket on my couch. I'll have it completely deconstructed soon. Can I sew it back together? Nope.

Malcolm was so great in Miami. Hell, he was great before Miami!

Then that same great guy somehow decided his next move should be to hang me in a restaurant with no warning. Never said a word. Just blew me up and had me nailed to the wall.

And what the hell did he tell my brother?

Another text. This is the third one. How can he honestly not know why I'm upset?

Did I say I wanted to be on display in Tara's restaurant? No. If he'd asked me, I would've said to tell her thanks, but no thanks. The photographer didn't even reach out to let me know he'd sold me. I know he didn't legally have to notify me. He owns the license. He had every right to sell it.

I just never imaged anyone would want to buy me. Especially not anyone I know!

It's creepy. No one expects to walk into a public place and see a highly edited version of herself floating at the end of a hallway.

Ellisandra is me, my favorite part of me, not a fictional rendering from an artist's imagination.

If Tara wanted a mermaid painting, she could've easily found one.

I'm real, and I'm not a fucking commodity. I'm not olive oil!

When I first looked at that photograph, I saw a professional image. One I could use to promote myself. Proudly and professionally.

Now, it's been edited to a fantasy. The mermaid in that baroque frame is a fanciful mythological creature. Unattainable. My own eyes staring back at me. Sirenic, yet derisive.

Aren't we lovely? Such a beautiful illusion.

I guess I should be grateful he didn't use me on his labels. Make me an actual part of his brand.

Great! He must've sent that last text from the parking lot of my apartments . . . because that's undeniably his knock. He won't go away if I ignore him.

I look at my phone and read that last message I ignored.

I'm here. On my way up.

There he goes again—just making decisions as if my opinion or feelings don't matter at all. He didn't ask if he could come up, just told me he was.

He knocks harder this time.

Oh, he really thinks he wants to talk to me face-to-face right now, huh? Hope he's ready.

I fling the door open and stare at him without a word.

"We should talk," he says.

Stepping aside, I give him the space to enter my apartment. I close the door behind him but still, I have nothing to say. When I headed for the door, a barrage of things I wanted to say was screaming in my head, but now, silence.

I expected him to immediately apologize and make excuses, but he looks mad, too.

"How could you have left, Ellis? You knew how important this event was, and you walked out on me. What did I do to deserve that?"

"I'm not olive oil!"

He blinks. Twice. Three times. "What?"

"Did you buy the picture or did Tara?"

"I did. It was a gift to celebrate the restaurant opening and to thank her for hosting my event."

"You thought that was fine. To just buy my photograph, have it altered to suit your needs, slap it in a giant, cheap, tacky frame and give it to your friend as a gift?"

"First of all, that frame is an antique, and it was not cheap. And it might not be your taste, but it is not tacky. Second of all . . . yes, of course, I thought it was fine. Why wouldn't it be fine?"

"Because I wasn't playing dress up when that picture was taken, Malcolm! It wasn't a photoshoot for mass production! I wasn't posing for a poster!"

"You're legitimately mad because that beautiful picture of you is hanging in a fine dining restaurant?"

"You don't respect my dream any more than my family does."

"Whoa, whoa, whoa! You know that's not true. I flew to Maimi to show my support. I tell you how much I believe in you all the time. How does buying that picture negate that?"

"She's just floating there with golden streaks in her hair and shimmery skin like some sort of fantasy creature. Trapped. Captured. Owned."

"That's how seeing that picture made you feel? Your insecurities are what this is really about?"

"Could you be a bigger asshole right now?"

"You have insecurities, Ellis. We all do. I can't tell you how to feel, but when I look at that picture, I don't see a possession. I feel inspired. You inspire me. You make me want to try harder, dream bigger. I don't think you're just a dreamer, I know you work hard and your goals are real, but you remind me that there's value in things other than bottom lines, that money isn't all that's worth striving for."

"You didn't need me to make you passionate about your job."

"No, but you make me remember that it's not just the oil in the bottle I'm passionate about. It's more than the finished product. It's the nurturing of the orchards, the people who do that work and the thousands of years of knowledge that's been passed down like folklore, the way they continue to expand on it and improve it, the millers who perfect the alchemy of turning fruit to oil, sometimes refusing new methods, not because they're too stubborn but because they know where the magic comes from."

"The romance of it." For the first time, I get it. Not just from his perspective, but I recognize it on my own.

"Exactly. And when I look at your picture edited and framed so beautifully on that wall, I see the romance of mermaiding. Yeah, maybe that includes the mythology and the fantasy, but isn't that part of the appeal even for you? Despite all the hard work and the uncertainty and the expenses and the fear of failure, something keeps you passionate about it."

"The romance." It's there for me, too.

"When I realized you were gone tonight, my heart broke. I carried on and got through it with a smile on my face because I had no choice, but my heart wasn't in it. I knew you were upset, but I didn't know why, and more importantly, I couldn't understand how you could walk out so easily."

"I run away when I'm hurt. If I can't escape the pain, I can at least escape the setting. If there's a pool to escape into, even better. It's how I coped growing up. That's why I spent so much time in the pool in our backyard. When the house got painful, I went underwater."

"You can't run from me like that, Ellis. You see it as an escape. I feel it as abandonment. If you're going to abandon me every time I do something that upsets you, this isn't going to work."

I want to run right now. My heart's hammering in my chest and my palms are sweating. "You can't just expect me to change who I am."

"Is that who you are though? Are you really someone who can't stay and face a problem, to talk things out, to show that even when you're angry or hurt, you won't leave?"

"I come back around, but I need space to work things out on my own first."

"No. I can respect your need for space after we talk, but I can't accept that you're going to run first. What happens when you decide not to come back around? When I'm conditioned to believe that you'll always come back, but one day, you just decide not to? Do you really believe you have a right to ask that of someone?"

"This isn't about me. This is about your parents. I can't heal that for you, Malcolm."

"I'm not asking you to heal it. I'm asking you to prove you're not going to repeat it."

"You're asking for a guarantee, and life doesn't come with guarantees."

"I'm asking you to love me. The way I deserve to be loved. Because I love you that way, and if you can't love me back in a way that allows for insecurities, then I don't think I'm the one asking for a guarantee."

"That's not fair, Malcolm. You can't throw down an ultimatum and call it love. You're right that it's wrong when I run so easily, okay? But I can't just flip a switch and change that about myself. You're asking me to trust you enough to stand and face things, but you're not willing to give me the space to develop that trust? That's not how relationships work."

"You don't trust me?"

"You're the one with the trust issues."

"Maybe some space would be good for both of us."

"Yeah. I think it would."

The moment he's gone, I collapse into a shaking, crying heap on my kitchen floor. No, no, no. It wasn't supposed to go like that. None of this was ever supposed to happen. We weren't supposed to hurt each other.

And that's not how he was supposed to say he loved me.

I wail. A howl echoes back.

Shut up, Meatball.

Following Passion
Malcolm

I TRY NOT TO look down the hallway when I go to bathroom. I could've avoided entering this hallway altogether if Emil hadn't insisted on meeting here for lunch.

He's Tara's wine supplier, and possibly something more as of recently, but if they don't want to go public with it yet, that's their business. I'll respect their privacy. I assume they have their reasons for wanting to keep it private, but if they don't stop looking at each other a certain way, they're going to out themselves. Pretty sure I'm not the only one who's noticing.

As I leave the bathroom, my eyes drift to her picture, and her beauty freezes me in my tracks. Not all secret relationships are meant to last, but goddamn, I miss her. How am I supposed to know how much space is enough? What are we missing out on in each other's lives for the sake of giving and respecting space?

If she got an audition, would she have told me? Or was I just a mistake she made for a while?

"How long are you going to keep torturing yourself?" Tara says as she walks up behind me. "If you're still that hooked on her, call her. Tell her!"

"She knows how I feel."

"How does she feel?"

"I honestly have no idea."

"Hmm, if only there were a way you could find out. A crystal ball maybe? Tea leaves? Tarot cards? A phone call!"

"Hey, don't yell at me. I know your secret."

"What secret? Me and Emil? We don't care who knows we're fucking."

"Oh. Well, damn. I misread that one."

"Assumptions are wrong more often than not, Malcolm. Call her."

Back in my office, I can't stop staring at the black and white photographs on my wall, pictures I took over ten years ago in Italy. I'm no photographer. They're not artistic shots by any means, but when I look at them, I see them through the eyes of that nineteen-year-old kid who couldn't believe he'd made it to Italy.

Those men with so much work to do, and only so much daylight to do it in, were so kind to me, so patient with the American boy, butchering their beautiful language because he couldn't hold back his questions, who interrupted their work over and over again for the sake of his own curiosity. His fascination.

They nurtured my budding obsession, generously sharing their knowledge. I could've learned on my own, but it would never have meant as much as being welcomed into their space. Maybe my interest made them feel seen while doing work that remains invisible to most people. Maybe sharing their work was good for them, too. I hope so.

I've always been a space invader, barging in uninvited wherever my curiosity spiked. I've matured, learned a hell of a lot since that first trip to Italy, but some situations don't have a clear right or wrong, no set-in-stone etiquette. Sometimes, you just have to let passion lead.

All That Glitters

Ellis

I HAVE NEVER BEEN more thankful to see someone's name pop up on a screen. I'm not even mad that she's calling instead of texting. When Sedona Rain calls, I answer. This is a mermaid opportunity, and I need one desperately right now. I tap the touchscreen on my dash to mute my music and take the call.

"Hey, Sedona."

"Hey. Do you have a minute?"

"Are you kidding? I'm sitting in Houston traffic. I have so many minutes."

"I don't know if you've heard yet, but there's been a shake up within the Fantasia Faeries Pod. It's been coming for a while, but it's all public now."

"No. I had no idea." This is not the kind of mermaid news I was hoping for. No wonder they haven't held auditions.

"I'm coming onboard."

"You're taking over the pod?"

"Not taking over. Becoming a partner. We've just cut three mermaids, and there was already technically an open spot. So, now there's four openings. What are you doing Saturday? As in next weekend, six days from now."

"Please tell me you're inviting me to audition."

"That's exactly what I'm doing. I know it's super short notice but it can't be helped. I've got some events coming up, and if I'm switching gears, I need to do it as quickly as possible. I think you're an amazing mermaid, Ellis. I wish I could tell you the decision was entirely up to me, but it's not. It's an invitation-only audition, but there will be more than four of you trying out. You swim beautifully. You've got great presence. I know what you bring to the water. Bring everything you've got to this audition. I'll send you the details."

"I'll be there. With everything I've got. Thank you!"

She ends the call, and I punch my steering wheel, accidentally honking. I wave sheepishly at the car in front of me so they know I wasn't honking at them in stop and go traffic. I'm not trying to incite a road rage incident, but I'd give anything to just blast my fucking horn and scream right now. If my car could shoot fireworks, I'd light up I-10 like the Fourth of July.

I've got an audition. And Sedona Rain is involved now. She knows me. We've worked together. The other five mermaids I worked with at the hotel opening in Miami were all great. What if we're all auditioning? Every mermaid who's ever worked for her is probably auditioning.

That waters down my excitement a little, but it's invitation-only, and with such short notice, how many mermaids could they have notified? Some of them probably won't even be able to make it.

I'm kidding myself. They'll all be there. Any mermaid looking to join a pod would do whatever it takes to accept an invitation like this. I wish she'd said exactly how many of us are auditioning. But I can't worry about the number. I've just got to focus on getting my wings.

This is it. This is my shot.

The last six weeks have been the absolute worst. I've been working nonstop to keep my mind off Malcolm. What I haven't been doing is training.

I've only got five days. I'm going to have to shuffle my schedule, make quite a few cancelations, and hit the pool twice a day.

And my dad is going to have to make peace with his fear of glitter. Theirs is the only pool where my tail is welcome. Semi-welcome, anyway. Mom hasn't banned it, and that pool is half hers.

Time to put together a basket of all Mom's favorite products from the spa.

Sorry, Dad. All's fair in love and your war on glitter.

I turn around and head right back for the parking garage I pulled out of twenty minutes ago. I'm rarely ever in the spa on a Sunday, let alone twice, but some things are worth doubling your trouble.

"What did I do to deserve all this?" Mom gushes over the basket. I may have gone a little overboard. Even with my employee discount, I had to put it on a credit card. Desperate times and all.

"I need you on my side about something."

"I'm always on your side. You don't have to bribe me." She dabs a new moisturizer on the back of her hand and rubs it in. "Oh, this feels nice."

"I got an audition with an elite mermaid pod. It could mean an actual steady income stream from mermaiding, but it's this Saturday."

"You'd really give up your other jobs for that? Honey, that seems risky."

"No, I'd still do freelance makeup artistry, and I'd still work part-time at the spa. You wouldn't lose your discount." I smile to reassure her. "But instead of doing those things more and mermaiding only occasionally, the time split would be the opposite. I'd do more mermaid work."

"Oh, good. I wouldn't want you to give up your other jobs to be a full-time mermaid. I'm not being critical, but sometimes things don't work out and you need something to fall back on."

"Right. But I don't have the spot yet. I have to audition. And I haven't been training like I should, so I need to use your pool. Twice a day for the next five days."

"You know you're always welcome to use the pool."

"For training. In my tail."

"Ohhhh."

"Please don't side with Dad if he starts about glitter in the pool. My tail doesn't even leave glitter in the pool, but he won't listen. This audition is really important to me."

"You know we won't be here, right? We're leaving tomorrow morning for that meteorology conference. He promised we could go on a river cruise next spring if I go with him to this thing. Brody is going to come over to feed the fish and clean the pool."

I look at the oversized basket of skincare products that I'll be paying interest on for the next six months. At least she'll have well-hydrated skin for the conference.

"I can do those things. Tell Brody he's off the hook."

"All right. Well, I guess things happen for a reason sometimes. The pool is all yours for the next five days."

"Thank you!" I throw my arms around her. This stroke of luck is worth two baskets of products.

"Do not leave glitter floating in the pool or clogging the filter, Ellis. Don't make me regret this."

On second thought, the one basket was plenty.

"I promise there will be no glitter in the pool, Mom."

Queso, Fries & Lies
Ellis

NEVER THOUGHT I'D BE living in this house again. It's only temporary, of course, but since I'm in the pool twice a day, it just makes sense to stay here. Plus, there's less chance I'll forget to feed Dad's fish, and I can bring in the mail.

Mom's not here to worry that I'm burning up her blender every time I make a smoothie, and Dad's not stressing about glitter in the pool. I've never been this comfortable here in my life. Full use of the pool, naps on the couch, no neighbors sharing the walls. It's great.

I just completed the third morning of my intense training. That's five sessions down; halfway there, and I can already feel the difference. When I finish my last session on Friday, I'll be so much better prepared for Saturday afternoon's audition. And I don't even have to fly.

They're holding auditions in Austin because Sedona's aunt owns a house with a pool big enough to audition mermaids, and on such short notice, there was no way she'd find a venue, anyway.

This audition feels charmed, like the stars aligned and everything fell into place perfectly. Like it was meant to be. I've got such a good feeling about this.

I'm meeting Maren for lunch, so no nap on the couch today. I go into Dad's office and give the fish a few shakes of food, careful not to give them too much. Watching these fish swim is my dad's relaxation therapy. And if anybody needs to relax, it's him.

"Are you getting excited?" Maren asked as she dips a trio of fries into the queso she ordered.

It's tormenting for me to watch her do that because I'm eating healthy this week. I haven't even had a single Oreo since Sunday.

"Getting excited? I've been excited since I got the invitation. Actually, I may be getting less excited, but in a good way, you know? Like, less anxious. More confident."

"You should be confident. You're the greatest mermaid in the whole world."

"You're the greatest friend in the whole world."

"Are you sure you don't want me to go with you? I could help you get in and out of your tail. Help you carry stuff. Come on. I've been your assistant before."

"No. I can't explain it, but I feel like I need to do this entirely on my own. But you'll be the first person I call when the auditions are over, I promise."

"We could make a girls' weekend of it, though. I wouldn't even have to go with you to the house for the auditions, but I'd be there when they were over, and we could spend Saturday night and Sunday having fun in Austin. We haven't gone out of town together in forever."

I know she wants to come in case I don't get chosen and I need a shoulder to cry on, and I love her for wanting to do that. And even more for not saying it out loud, but I need to do this entirely solo.

She waves a fry dripping with queso toward me like a bribe. It's so enticing, but if I wanted some of her fries and queso, I'd just help myself. But I won't because I don't give in to self-sabotage that easily. Not anymore. I shake off the offer.

"Geez, you've got good self-control."

"I have to be disciplined. Trust me, it's not easy." I look down at my lettuce-wrapped burger and my tastebuds water at the thought of having it on a giant, soft brioche bun like the one Maren's having. Maybe next week, but not today.

"Are you still avoiding that doctor you brought to the launch party?" I ask in an attempt to lob some misery back at her.

"I was doing so well, but then I had to organize a meeting for the owner and all the doctors and nurses on staff, and I obviously couldn't avoid him at that. Then after the meeting, he asked if I wanted to grab a drink, and so we did . . . that was on Monday."

"And?"

"And drinks turned into dinner."

"And dinner turned into?"

"Don't ask questions you already know the answer to."

"Why are you so resistant to dating him? He's cute. He seemed nice. He's a doctor!"

"When have I ever dated anyone that conventional? I date musicians and bartenders, guys who are fun. Not doctors and lawyers."

"He's on staff for a chain of cryotherapy centers, Maren. How conventional can he be?"

"I know. He's a partner in an integrative medicine practice, not the most traditional western medicine doc, but still."

"Still what?"

"I don't want to be my mom, chasing wealthy men and status. Those things don't matter to me."

"I'm not sure Beth has ever been the one doing the chasing. And it doesn't sound like you're the one doing the chasing either. Besides, the last *bartender* you dated was a bar owner. He owned six bars if I remember correctly? That man was wealthy, Maren."

"But he started out as a bartender."

"So did a lot of doctors and lawyers."

"Don't be rational when I need you to be irrational with me."

"That's my line."

"Yeah, well, friends share."

"You're right." I steal a fry and dip it into her queso. Just one.

"Have you still not talked to him at all, El?"

"No. I told you, we're done. It was fun while it lasted. Did I tell you he signed me up for his olive oil subscription box? The first one arrived last Friday."

"Did it have good stuff in it?"

"Yes, of course. That's so manipulative though. He only did it to make me think about him."

"He's obviously still thinking about you."

"We were never meant to last. And it would've ended in disaster if Brody had found out. It's better that it just fizzled out on its own. This way, nobody got hurt."

"You are so full of shit."

"Stop making me eat fries!"

Better Alone
Malcolm

HER CAR HASN'T BEEN home at night all week, but maybe she'll be here in the middle of the day on a Wednesday.

It's still not here. She could be out of town for work, on location for a film somewhere. I know she's done that before. Or maybe her car's in the shop.

What I'm about to do will never leave the sacred confines of my car. I pull into a parking spot in front of her apartment to make the call.

"Thank you for calling Willowscape Spa. This is Breanna. How may I help you today?"

"Hi, Breanna. Um, so, my girlfriend's birthday is next week, and I wanted to book an appointment for her as a surprise. I think she sees Emma. No, that's not right. Ella?"

"Ellis?"

"Yeah, that's it. Thanks. Does she have any openings this week?"

Damn, I'm good at this.

"No, I'm sorry. Ellis is out all week. She'll be back in the spa next Tuesday. Would you like me to check for her first available appointment?"

Shit. She really is out of town.

"No, that's fine. Thanks, anyway."

"I could have Ellis give you a call. Is this a good number?"

"What? No, no, really, there's no need. I'll call again when she's back in the office. The spa."

Holy fuck. I didn't think about my number showing up.

"If you'd like to buy your girlfriend a gift certificate instead, I can help you with that. If you tell me her name, I can pull up her profile and give you a price for her usual services."

"Actually, I think she's only been there once. I'm not even sure Ellis is the right name now that I think about it. Thanks for your help."

I have never ended a call so fast in my life. I didn't know I was going to be interrogated. Where'd they find that receptionist, the CIA? Man, she's relentless. I still have no idea where Ellis is, but I know she'll be back by Tuesday.

Something Brody said a few days ago replays in my head. His parents are away at a conference this week. Would she have gone with them? No. That's stupid. Why would she have gone with them?

But what if she's housesitting? Maybe she took the week off to just lay around the pool and relax. She was working a lot. Everybody needs a break eventually.

My heart rate kicks up a little. Hope.

It's funny how hope can bloom so quickly and be crushed even quicker. Her car's not at her parents' place either.

I probably wouldn't have knocked on the door, anyway. But I would've felt better, knowing where she was.

This sucks. I can't ask Brody about her, and I don't know Maren well enough to reach out to her and ask. It's not like she's missing. The spa knew she was going to be out this week. She cleared her schedule. The truth is it's none of my business where she is.

I just thought she might've reached out after she got the box to say thanks, or fuck off. Something. Anything. But I got nothing.

My schedule's clear for the rest of the day, so I head home. To stare at my computer screen. I can't do nothing at all or my mind will wander right back to her.

Tara and Emil have floated the idea of doing monthly events at her newest restaurant, the one where the most beautiful mermaid floats at the end of the hall. He and I would partner to pair olive oils and wines. Her chef would curate a full menu for us to accentuate throughout the evening. I've been weighing the potential benefits, thinking of some oils I might like to feature.

The idea's not terrible. I'm just not sure I want to commit to any type of partnership right now, not even an unofficial one.

I'm in sort of a lone wolf phase, I guess. I don't really want to work with anyone, or even see people as much as I used to. It's been too hot to ride my board to the office, so I've been working from home more.

Aside from the moments when memories of her rip my guts out, I get a lot done. Some days, I don't even get dressed. It's great.

Rolling in the Deep
Ellis

I MAY HAVE PUSHED myself a little too hard in the pool this evening. But I only have four sessions left after today. I've got to make the most of them.

All Maren's Malcolm sympathizing left my stomach feeling sour after lunch. That's probably contributing to the weakened way I feel tonight, too.

It doesn't matter if I like knowing he's thinking about me. Malcolm's basically a nice person. Sending me the subscription box was probably just his way of saying he didn't mean to hurt me. A truce of sorts. We hurt each other, but I don't have any covert way of letting him know I didn't mean it either.

I'm the one who asked for space.

Not just me. He said it was a good idea, too.

We might have to see each other again someday. Brody and Amanda want kids, and he'll be at every birthday party. I'll have to share every important event in my niece or nephew's life with him. He'll upstage me with every birthday present. Probably take the kid to Italy!

He'll be Uncle Mal. I'll be Aunt Ellie. And no one but the two of us will ever know what we once were to each other. For a little while. A really good little while.

I need to eat.

The moment I open my mom's pantry, I see the bottle. He must've signed them up for the subscription box, too. Or maybe they joined on their own. That seems like the kind of thing my dad would do. Quietly show support he'd never admit out loud.

Not for me, but he'd probably do something like that for Malcolm.

When I decide on pasta for dinner, the oil is just a logical choice. I pour a little onto my fingertip and taste it. Grassy, but buttery. Peppery on the end. Definitely costs more than eight bucks a bottle.

I laugh at the memory of Malcolm throwing out my possibly fake olive oil. He threw out nearly everything in my fridge.

And then he brought me real olive oil.

Then even better oil.

Taught me how to taste it. How to waste it—without a single fucking regret. That afternoon will forever live rent-free in my head, and it will remain one of the greatest sexual experiences of my life.

Along with the first time he spanked me, the way he understood without me having to explain it at all. Hell, he understood it better than I did. There was a lot about me that he understood. But the things he didn't . . .

We didn't understand everything about each other, weren't as compatible as we'd thought.

I'm probably not the first person to cry while eating this high-protein pasta. It's not good. It tastes sad. Chewy and grainy and sad. There should be a warning on the box that says you shouldn't eat this if you're already feeling down because it will push your emotions right over the fucking edge. I hate this shitty sad pasta.

But I don't want to waste this incredible oil. It's really good. And I have to eat.

Mom's wine selection is tempting in the same way Maren's queso and fries were, but I can't give in to it.

I can't just sit here, crying at the kitchen table all night either. The pool needs to be cleaned. Of leaves and bugs, not glitter. Cleaning the pool will force me to move, loosen up my muscles. I put my bowl in the dishwasher and get the pool skimmer from the shed.

There's something almost hypnotic about cleaning the pool in the dark. The lights under the water make it glow. Flies that are incessantly annoying by day float silently on the surface with their holographic wings shimmering. Fallen live oak leaves that have been blown into the pool rock like tiny trolling jon boats.

Why didn't we always do this after dark? It's almost magical.

Pulling the net through the water, I make another slow trip around the edge, watching the ripples fan out. A dragonfly skims the surface. I pause to let it cool off without feeling threatened. It hovers in the light for a moment before it takes flight again.

My eyes track it across the yard and over the gate as it opens.

Who is opening the gate?

"What are you doing here?"

"Saw your car out front."

"Why are you in this neighborhood?"

"Just driving around. I rang the doorbell. When you didn't answer, I thought I might find you in the pool."

"I'm not in it. Just cleaning it."

"So you can get in it without bugs sticking to you?"

"No." I laugh because I used to ask Brody to skim the bugs when I wanted to swim at night. I'd forgotten that sometimes Malcolm would do it if Brody said no. "I'm done swimming for the day."

"Are you sure about that?"

"Yeah. My muscles are all exhausted."

"Oh. If your body's that tired, it would be a shame if you fell in."

"Don't even think about it. I mean it, Malcolm. Stop right there."

"If you accidentally fall in, I just want to be close enough to rescue you."

I raise the pool skimmer in front of my body. "I swear to Neptune, I will lay your ass out with this."

"Really? You're gonna lay my ass out with that plastic stick, huh?"

"I'm not playing."

He keeps advancing. The gate is the only way out of the back-yard, and I'd have to run right past him to get to it. I wouldn't make it to the back door without him catching me either.

"I can't believe you'd threaten someone who's just here to rescue you."

"I don't need rescuing."

"But you might."

"Don't come any closer. I'll scream."

I take a step back.

He takes a step forward.

I retreat another step, and my back foot comes down on air . . . and keeps going. My front leg locks, trying to secure my balance. The pool skimmer tips to the right and the weight of the basket pulls me to side with it. I wobble, holding onto the handle as long as I can, right up until the exact second that I know if I don't drop it, I'm going to . . .

Dammit!

Malcolm dives into the water right behind me.

He has his arms around me before I can swim out of his reach.

We come up for air, both sputtering and blinking.

"See?" he says. "It's a good thing I was here."

"You're the reason I fell!"

"I didn't even touch you."

"Not yet, but you were threatening to."

"Who was threatening who? You were the one wielding a pool skimmer like a sword. What was it you were going to do again? Lay my ass out, I think was how you put it."

"Yeah, until you made me fall into the pool."

"Shut up and kiss me."

"It's not nice to tell someone to shut up."

"I'm not a nice guy."

"Yes, you are. It's your biggest flaw."

"Well, damn, now I'm curious to know what you think my good qualities are."

"Maybe I don't think you have any."

"Okay. I'll tell you yours instead. You're so goddamn stubborn you make me have to knock you into a pool to get your attention. The thought of being in love scares the hell out of you. And you give up too fucking easy."

"I thought you were going to list my good qualities."

"Oh, these are your good qualities."

"Let go of me."

"Not yet. You're stubbornly guarded because you are so fiercely independent, which would be sexy as hell if there was a reasonable limit to it. If you'd just trust enough to let someone in without being afraid that they were going to take over your whole life. You're afraid to admit it when you love someone because if it doesn't work out, they might get hurt. And the truth is you care more about other people's feelings than you do your own. That's the same reason you'll give up without a fight. Someone might get hurt. But that's a pointless thing to fear, Ellis. Someone will definitely get hurt. Love is gonna hurt sometimes. But denying it's not pain-free either. Is it?"

"No." I blink back tears. "You can stop talking and kiss me now."

I expect a sweeping, romantic kiss, but he cuts it short.

"You taste like really good olive oil."

"You taste like this might be a mistake."

"You love making mistakes."

"How would you ever know if I really cared about you, or I was just hanging around for the free olive oil?"

"I'll start charging you for the oil."

"But I'll get a discount, right?"

"You can name your price, Buttercup."

"I'm still not sure about this. I mean, I remembered you being a way better kisser."

His next kiss is the one I was expecting. I could float forever on this kiss.

"What the fuck?" His voice rises over the sound of the back door flying open so hard it hits the side of the house.

"Brody? What are you doing here?"

"Mom asked me to come by and feed Dad's fish."

"She was supposed to tell you not to worry about that. But it's day three. They have to be fed every day! Tonight is seriously the first time you've remembered to come feed them?"

"I came by this afternoon and fed them. But I forgot the bag from my lunch. Dad would have a damn fit if he came home and found my three-day-old fast-food trash in his office. So I came back over to throw it away. And I find you like this!"

"You weren't planning to come back and feed them again? Wait a minute. I fed them today, too. Oh, shit. We're going to kill Dad's fish."

"I don't give a fuck about the fish. But I'm going to kill you, asshole." He points at Malcolm. "Get out of the pool."

"Fuck you, Brody. I'm not getting out of the damn pool."

"Get off my sister!"

"We're really doing this, huh?" Malcolm lets me go and swims toward the edge.

Amanda runs after Brody, trying to hold him back. "You don't want to fight Malcolm!"

"Yes, I do!" He keeps storming for the pool, pulling Amanda along behind him.

She holds tight to his arm with both hands. "Brody, stop and think about this before you do something you're going to regret."

"Listen to your wife!" I yell.

"You shut up, Ellis! I'll deal with you later."

"Don't fucking tell her to shut up!" Malcolm pushes himself up on the side of the pool.

"Deal with me later?" I yell. "How about you deal with me now?" I swim for the edge, too.

"Ellis, you're not helping," Amanda says, still clutching Brody's arm.

He lurches forward as hard as he can and shirks her grip, but it sends him stumbling for a few feet. Malcolm grabs his ankle and yanks.

And now they're both in the pool, grappling and grabbing like a couple of idiots.

I get out and walk to Amanda, who is staring in disbelief at the scene taking place in the pool. Brody and Malcolm are throwing wet punches in between holding each other under the water.

"What are we going to do?" Her voice is frantic. She didn't grow up with a brother. She thinks they might actually kill each other.

"I'm going to have a glass of wine. Want to join me?"

She hesitates, but then she follows me to the back door, glancing over her shoulder every few steps.

It sounds like they're taking a break from trying to drown each other. They're screaming like lunatics now. One of the neighbors may call the cops any minute.

The thrashing begins again.

"They'll come in when they've tired themselves out."

"Are you sure?"

"This isn't the first time they've had a fight in that pool."

"Yeah, but it's the first time for this reason. I don't know if we should leave them, Ellis. Brody really might drown someone for you."

"He won't. He's smarter than he looks." I go inside to strip down and dry off. I wrap a towel around my body. After I've dried up my wet trail through the kitchen, I open the wine.

Amanda comes in a few minutes later. "They're yelling again."

"Yelling is good. Means they're both still alive." I pass her a glass of wine. "Lock the door. I don't want them bringing that shit in here."

"How are you so calm about this?"

"This is only the second most alarming thing that has happened to me tonight. I'm still trying to recover from the first."

"Are you okay?"

"Yeah. I'm good. I think."

We sit at the table and sip our wine, taking turns cracking the door open to check for signs of life. They're still alive, still going strong.

When they finally stagger to the back door, soaked and wheezing, I shake my head at them through the glass.

Brody tries the handle. "Open this door, Ellis!"

"No. You'll drip pool water all over the floor. There are towels in the deck box."

He hurls the lid to the deck box across the yard. It lands in the pool. His towel gets hung on something, forcing him to wrestle it free. Malcolm pulls one out with less of a struggle, but his jaw is still clenched. They're not cooled off enough to come inside yet.

I pour myself another glass of wine. I'll feel it during my training tomorrow morning, but my nerves don't care tonight.

The guys sit on patio chairs and stare at the sky. There is an occasional eruption of raised voices, shaking heads, and flailing arms, but no new punches are thrown.

Eventually, I let them in. Malcolm comes straight to my side and puts his arm around my waist.

Brody glares at him. Malcolm glares back.

Amanda and I exchange smiles. "Okay," she says. "Let's go home before you give the neighbors any more of a wild story to tell your parents."

"I want to talk to my sister." He looks at Malcolm. "You should go."

"I'm not going anywhere."

"Goddammit, Malcolm! If I tell you to get out of my house, you have to leave!"

"No, he doesn't," I say. "It's my house, too."

Amanda laughs heartily now. "Neither of you lives here anymore. It's your parents' house. Is this what it was like when y'all were growing up?"

Malcolm answers for us. "Yes. This is exactly what they were like. They fought constantly, but always defended each other if anyone else got involved."

"I'm not defending him," I say.

"I know. But he believes he's defending you."

"I don't need him to defend me."

"I know that, too. But he thinks he's doing the right thing."

"Quit trying to explain me to my own sister!" Brody's face is turning red again.

"That's it!" Amanda yells. "We're leaving. Now." She pulls on Brody's arm again.

"I'm not leaving until he does."

"He's staying." I stiffen my spine and stare down my brother.

"Why, Ellis? Why him?"

"He has a better beard than any of your other friends."

Malcolm and Amanda both laugh. Brody doesn't.

"You think this is funny?"

"Go home, Brody."

He follows Amanda to the front door, but he glances back over his shoulder before they leave and says, "We are going to have a serious talk about this, Ellis."

"Okay. Goodnight."

When the door closes behind them, Malcolm says, "Can I really stay?"

"Oh, you're not walking out and leaving me like this."

Tearing Down Walls
Malcolm

"I'm not sure I can do this in your childhood bedroom. Maybe we should go back outside." I look at the bookshelf full of mermaids her mom has left intact. So many eyes watching.

"The neighbors have enough to report to my parents." She drops her towel.

What mermaids?

"God, I've missed you. Missed this sweet mouth." I pull her close and resume the kiss her brother interrupted earlier. My hands go straight to her ass, squeezing and kneading. "Missed this ass for sure."

"It's missed your hands."

"When did you become such a dirty little temptress?"

"I became a lot of things while you weren't looking."

"In my defense, you weren't around for me to look at."

"You're the one who ran off to Italy."

"You wouldn't have wanted me before I did that."

"I wasn't done becoming all the things you'd want before then either. Not for a long while after."

"Good thing we took our time."

"Well, yeah. Good timing is like our signature thing."

"Nobody does it better."

"Shut up and spank me."

I walk her to the bed. "Face down, ass up, Buttercup."

She slowly shakes her head no, and then she points to the mattress. "Have a seat."

Is she actually going to lay across my lap? My dick twitches at the thought. We can do this however she wants. But please, God, let her be coordinating the image in my head.

When she drapes her gorgeous body over my knees, I run my hand down her back from her shoulder blades to her tailbone and back up again. She is warm and soft, and I just need to touch her, to feel the tension leave her body. This won't fully do it for her, but it starts the process.

I watch my hand glide down again, dip at her lower back, and rise over the curve of her ass.

She squirms on my lap, and I know damn well what she wants, but I'm not ready to give it to her yet. Not ready to take that much liberty with her body yet, either. Timing.

"What did you miss about me?" I ask.

I expect a sarcastic response, but she takes my breath away when she says, "I missed feeling safe. I didn't feel unsafe in the world before you, but when you were gone, I was afraid of things that hadn't scared me in a really long time. You tore down walls I worked so hard to build. I was left unprotected and angry at myself because I'd let it happen."

"Let what happen?"

"Let myself fall in love with you."

My hand brushes her hair off her shoulders, completely exposing her to me. She tenses a little again when she is fully bare.

"Were you angry at me for loving you, too?"

"Yeah. And for the way you made me trust."

"But you didn't really trust me. You admitted that."

"You made me trust myself. And then I fucked up. If I hadn't let my guard down, I wouldn't have let myself get so emotional. Not about a photograph. Or anything else."

I continue to rub her back, to trace her vertebrae and palm her ass without breaking contact. She writhes as my hand approaches her lower back again. Being physically vulnerable like this turns her on, but the emotional vulnerability is still hard.

"I didn't understand your reaction at the time, but looking back, I like that you freaked out, fucked up, to use your words. You can fuck up and be emotional with me, Ellis. About anything. I'd take that any day over you keeping parts of yourself hidden from me. I don't want to know you on a surface level. I want all your walls torn down."

"I'm just not good at letting go like that."

"You can let go. I know you can."

I slap her ass, and her whole body tightens from the surprise. She swans her spine and whimpers when I spank her again. My handprint turns a brighter shade of pink on her skin. Small welts rise after a few more slaps . . . and then she lets go, her body softening on my lap, a quiet moan leaving her lips. There she is, exactly where she needs to be.

Letting everything else go.

My fingers tease the seam of her pussy. I smile as she rocks her hips up to coax me closer to her opening. She has more power over me than she knows. Or maybe she's well aware. I don't mind.

And I couldn't keep my fingers out of her sweet little snatch right now if I wanted to. She's tight and so damn wet. I circle her clit until it swells enough that she inches away from my touch when I get too close. It wouldn't take much at all to make her come, but I want her in a much more vulnerable position, one where she can't bury her face in my leg to muffle her sounds.

I want my face to be the one that's buried.

"Get on the bed." She doesn't hesitate, but she attempts to comply with my original request, face down and ass up. "No. On your back. Legs spread."

Again, no argument. I watch her get into position while I undress. "Wider."

Her legs butterfly a little more, but her knees are bent with her feet planted.

When I climb onto the bed, I gently press against her knees to lay them flat, take her ankles and shove them higher. This is how I want her, stretching her limits and hiding nothing from me.

I kiss my way up her inner thigh, and she wiggles when my beard tickles her skin. When I lick her for the first time, she takes a sharp inhale, but her exhale comes out on a long, mewling moan that makes my balls draw up tight and my mouth smile against her slickness.

If she only knew how well she lets go for me.

After she's bucked her way through an orgasm so intense it's soaked not only my beard, but also her comforter, I smile up at her and say, "It's your turn to choose. Pick any position you want."

She smiles back at me with her eyelids heavy and her cheeks flushed, and then she rolls over.

Her ass is still red, and her clit's still too tender to touch, but her drenched pussy takes every inch of my dick like we were made for each other. I could fuck this woman for the rest of my life.

Hopes and Schemes
Ellis

I WAKE UP WITH Malcolm's heavy leg slung across my body. My sheets smell like sex and chlorine.

Yeah, nobody's buying that candle, but there's no point in showering since I need to get up and hit the pool.

He protests when I shift under his leg.

"You have to let me up. I've got to train."

"Perfect. I'll be your coach. I just need coffee first."

"I don't need a coach."

"And I don't like the idea of you training in the pool all alone. It's dangerous."

"Just my style."

"Styles change." He sits up, yawns, and rubs his eyes.

"I forgot what a pain the ass you can be."

"I haven't even been in your ass yet. But if that was an invitation . . ."

I leap out of the bed before he can trap me again. "It's entirely too early for anal."

"In the morning or in the relationship?"

"Go get yourself some coffee. Bring me back a large iced mocha and put it in the fridge so I'll have something to look forward to after I get out of the pool."

"What am I, chopped liver? You could look forward to me when you get out of the pool."

"I'll be looking forward to an iced mocha."

I hit him in the face with a pillow. He doesn't even try to block it, just laughs, and then groans when he stands up. "You need a new mattress."

"Cool. I'll pass your request on to my mom."

"No, you won't. That would implicate you, too."

"You know they have a doorbell cam, right? She's going to know you spent the night here."

"Fuck me. I'm sure that would've occurred to me at some point, but couldn't you have just left me blissfully ignorant for a little while longer?"

"She'll know Brody and Amanda were here, too. I'll tell her we all had a few drinks. You had a few too many, and crashed on the couch."

"Yeah, that'll really help my image with your dad."

"Well, if you'd rather I tell them the truth . . . why are you staring at me like that?"

"The way you just wiggled into those bathing suit bottoms is making me rethink my mattress complaint."

"Tie the back strings for me." I hold my top against my chest and turn so he can reach the strings hanging at my sides.

"Now you're just being mean."

"Go. Follow the siren song of the coffee shop."

"Don't get in the pool until I get back."

"No promises."

"I guess I'll drive fast and hope for the best."

"Hoping for the best is always a good plan." I adjust my top and kiss him on the cheek. "Some guy with a great beard and an amazing dick taught me that."

Two hours later, I'm barely able to hoist myself up and out of the pool. I roll onto my stomach. "Unzip me, please!" I yell, slapping my tail on the pavement.

Malcolm stops typing on his laptop and sets it on the patio table long enough to help me free my legs.

I shower. He showers.

We nap.

He works some more while I push through my afternoon training session, and then he goes out to pick up dinner.

While he's gone, I call my sister-in-law.

"Hey, Amanda. How do you feel about hosting a surprise joint thirtieth birthday party?"

"Well, that would be one way to force them together again."

"Got any ideas for a venue?"

"What about Vegas? They were supposed to go together to celebrate their birthdays. They'd never suspect we were planning a party for them there."

"That's perfect!"

"You know we'd have to invite your parents, right?"

"I honestly can't think of a better place to unleash Mallis on them."

"That couple name couldn't be any more perfect for y'all."

"Right? Sounds sinister, but it's really adorable. It's totally us. Once everyone gets over the initial shock, they'll see."

"Well, this could only go one of two ways."

"Hope for the best, Amanda. Hope for the best."

Learning New Tricks
Malcolm

I LAY HER TAIL across her backseat. "I really wish you'd let me come with you to Austin."

"I can't. I told Maren no, so I have to tell you no, too."

"Do Maren and I have all the same permissions?"

She pats my chest. "Put that fantasy out of your head, big guy. Or at least be smart enough not to ever mention it again."

"Let me know as soon as you get there."

"I will. And I'll see you at the airport tomorrow morning. If I'm a Fantasia Faerie, we'll drink champagne in the bar. If I'm not, we'll drink tequila. Either way, we will be Vegas bound to celebrate your senior citizenship." She tugs on my beard to pull me close enough for a kiss.

"We'll have two reasons to celebrate. I can feel it."

"That's my ass you're feeling, and you need to let it go so I can get on the road."

She cranks her music up as she pulls away from the curb in front of her parents' house. I can still hear it after she turns at the corner. It's not safe to drive with it that loud. She won't be able to hear an emergency vehicle coming up behind her or another car honking their horn . . . shit, maybe I am a senior citizen.

There are a lot of things I thought I'd be by thirty. Hopelessly in love with Ellis French was not one of them.

I drive home, hop on my board, and head into the office. It's quiet on a Saturday. This is when I used to get some of my best work done. Today, I can't stop checking the time on my phone.

Ellis finally lets me know she's there at ten-thirty, which is right on schedule. She's there, so I should be able to relax now. But I'm going insane because I'm not there with her. I really think she's going to get a spot, and when she does, she'll be surrounded by other mermaids she can celebrate with. She deserves this space to soak up her accomplishment with her colleagues. If she doesn't make it, there will be mermaids there to console her, too.

She doesn't need me for this. I hate that. I want her to need me for everything, but that's my issue, not hers.

I'm working on it. I may be working on it forever, but for her, I'll keep trying.

Auditions are going to last into the evening. I can't just sit here checking my phone every five minutes for the next eight hours.

I ride over to the skate park to distract myself. A kid who reminds me way too much of myself at that age asks how old I am. When I tell him I'm turning thirty tomorrow, he spares no emotion in letting me know how impressed he is that "an old dude" like me still skates. I would've said that to me at his age, too.

Still kind of want to trip him, but I laugh and tell him I'm sure he'll be able to skate when he's thirty.

He tells me his best friend doesn't skate, but they're still cool.

Wish I could guarantee him that would still be true when he turned thirty.

Brody was supposed to be going to Vegas this weekend, too. He's still twenty-nine until Wednesday, but we've celebrated our birthdays together since we were about the same age as the mouthy little shit trying to perfect a kickflip.

"Your feet are too close together. And you're not jumping high enough."

"Really?"

I demonstrate, once again blowing his young mind. "Spread your feet. Shed your fear. You'll land it."

He tries again, nails it, and pumps his fist in the air. "Hell, yeah. Thanks, old dude!"

I laugh along with him. And then I flip him off. He returns the salute. I skate home before I get too cocky and break something.

I've got a flight I can't miss tomorrow.

When in Doubt, Carb Out
Ellis

IT'S GOT TO BE a good sign that I'm being asked to roll into the pool again. Controlled splash. I've entered the water perfectly four times now.

Sedona Rain calls two more names and tells them she needs to see their barrel rolls again.

I'm called back for a second look at my flip.

Then three other mermaids are asked to flip again.

We swim the length of the pool in pairs. For the third time.

There are only nine of us here. But only four spots, so that means more of us are being told no than yes. That's always the case at an audition, but it feels especially tense with so few of us trying out.

I don't know how long we've been going, but it's been hours, and I'm tired. We all are.

I'd rather be called back into the pool repeatedly than wait on the side, though. The waiting is the worst.

Viviana, the original owner of the Fantasia Faeries steps to the side of the yard to confer and compare notes with Sedona. Lots of head nodding and whispering. The pool is surrounded by nervous mermaids.

Sedona and Viviana come back to the pool area.

"Thank you, mermaids," Sedona says. "I know we've asked a lot of you today, and we appreciate your patience. Auditions are over."

What? That's it?

Viviana steps forward. "As the founder of the Fantasia Faeries, I want to express my sincere gratitude to each of you for coming out on such short notice. Your enthusiasm and love for mermaiding is evident, and it means the world to me that you want to be a part of something so dear to my heart."

The new partners exchange a look, and Sedona says, "We'll be notifying everyone tomorrow evening. If you are not chosen, you will receive a text and an email. If your phone rings, please answer it so we can congratulate you and welcome you to the pod. Drive safe, everyone."

With that, she and Viviana walk into the house and leave us to gather our tails and go.

There is some grumbling around the pool. But they never actually said they'd let us know today. I guess we all just assumed since we were scrambling on such short notice, the decisions would be made immediately. And announced immediately.

I really wish I'd brought someone with me now. If I asked Malcolm to come, he'd probably drive up, but that would be ridiculous. We're flying out of Houston tomorrow. Maren would come, too, but we wouldn't have time to do anything. I'm leaving early in the morning to make that flight to Vegas.

So, it'll be just me, tossing and turning in a hotel bed all night long. All alone. I'm suddenly feeling like not the smartest mermaid in the ocean.

With my tail hanging in the shower and my stomach still doing barrel rolls, I order a burger from room service—on the biggest bun they offer. Carb-loading before three days in Vegas can't be a bad idea.

I'm still a little shocked my parents accepted the invitation. I really thought they'd say no since they've just been gone for a week, but apparently, they're more than willing to jump through hoops to be at their son's thirtieth birthday party in Vegas.

They've been home for hours and Mom still hasn't texted to ask why Malcolm was there overnight. That seems suspicious. Maybe she's just busy doing their laundry and repacking.

Dad's fish were all still alive when I left. I wonder who's going to feed them while we're all in Vegas. Probably someone who won't get into a fight in their pool or have sex in my old room. But the bugs have been skimmed and the sheets are clean, just in case.

Hopefully, their neighbors won't have time to narc on us before they head out again tomorrow.

I finish off my burger with a yawn. Holding my eyes open becomes a struggle. Carbs were definitely the right idea.

Into the Wild West
Malcolm

A FEW DAYS AWAY with Ellis is exactly what I need. It's what we need. I know she's disappointed about the delay in the audition results, but I like that I'll get to be with her when she finds out.

She should be here by now, though. I'm not getting off this bench until she's here and we can go through security together. I don't have a bag to check, just a carry-on, but I bet she'll need to check one. If she doesn't show up soon—

"Why do you look so stressed out?"

"It's about time you got here."

She sits on my lap and kisses me. This is an awful lot of public affection for her. Not that I'm complaining. "Happy Birthday!" she yells loudly enough to attract way too much attention.

Several people walking by also wish me a happy birthday.

"Let's get your bag checked and get to our gate."

Once we're through security, I relax a little, despite Ellis telling everyone around us, including the TSA agents that it's my birthday. I'm pretending not to be bothered by it because she's having fun.

I'd forgotten how much she loves birthdays. Everyone's birthday.

We make it into the terminal with plenty of time to spare, and this is exactly how I like it. She pulls me into a bar.

"We don't know the answer yet," I say. "How do we know what to drink?"

"Champagne. We're manifesting."

"Of course we are." I hate champagne, but I'll have a few sips for her.

We toast to the inevitable good news.

Vegas is scorching, but it's freezing in the hotel. All or nothing. Welcome to Sin City.

"Let's take a nap," Ellis says as soon as we get into our room.

"Just a nap?"

"Blowjob and a nap?"

"Happy Birthday to me."

I wake to Ellis pulling the curtains open, letting the late afternoon sun blaze into the room. "Time to go to dinner," she says.

"It's four o'clock. That's too early for dinner."

"Not on your birthday. Come on, let's go."

"I didn't know I was coming to birthday bootcamp."

"I don't think people get champagne and blowjobs at bootcamp."

"Probably not the champagne, anyway."

The sound of her laughter puts me in an instant good mood. Fine. She wants to go to dinner at four o'clock, we'll go to dinner.

We've barely finished dessert when she insists we should go back to our hotel and have a drink in the bar there.

"Let's go to the casino instead."

"No, not tonight. We can do casinos tomorrow night."

"We're going to spend all night in the hotel bar?"

She stares at me for a minute, and I swear, I can see the gears turning in her brain. "The night's young. Who knows where it might lead?"

"You're acting strange. Stranger than usual."

"I'm excited for your birthday." She chews her bottom lip. "And nervous about the results."

Shit. I should've realized she's trying to keep busy so she won't worry about that. I'll go with any strange choice she makes tonight. She looked at her phone half a dozen times during dinner.

"You're right. Let's go have a drink at the hotel and see where the night leads."

When I head for the door of our hotel, she pulls me back. "No, not this door. There's another one around the corner that's closer to the bar. We're supposed to use that one."

"Supposed to? It's a thousand degrees out here. Let's use this one."

"No, Malcolm. We can't."

"Why not?"

Again, I get that same vacant stare she gave me in the restaurant.

"It's bad luck. You have to indulge all my superstitions tonight, okay?"

"The door around the corner is better luck?"

"Yes. If we go through this one and then I get bad news . . ."

"Okay. Okay. It's hard to argue with you when you're wearing my favorite little green dress."

"This dress makes you weak?"

"It might make me stupid. But let's go through the door that can't hurt your chances of becoming a fairy mermaid."

"Thank you." She takes my hand and swings our arms as we walk. "It's his birthday," she tells a bachelorette party on the sidewalk. A chorus of drunken happy birthday wishes follows.

"Stop telling people it's my birthday."

"I will. Tomorrow."

When we're finally back inside, she won't let me order at the bar, again pulling me in another direction. "I'll find us a good table."

I follow along, watching my favorite dress cling to her body as she walks. When I look up, I do a doubletake. That guy looks just like . . . it is Emil.

There's Tara. Maren is standing next to a woman who looks enough like her that I know she must be the infamous Beth who I've heard so much about. And Ellis's parents are right behind them. My mom's here, too?

I look around to see more faces I recognize, and then Brody and Amanda walk in from the lobby, where the door I wasn't allowed to use would've led me.

As it sinks in, Brody and Amanda come closer. She and Ellis throw their arms up in victory, and the crowd yells, "Surprise!"

There's a good chance I've never been more surprised in my life. How the hell did they pull this off? Why?

"Are you surprised?" Ellis asks.

She's so happy. I can't tell her there's no way this is going to live up to her expectations.

"I am extremely surprised."

Everyone is laughing and hugging. They are all thrilled to have surprised us. Brody and I make eye contact, but he's quick to look away. Yeah, this was a bad idea.

It's fine. I'll just stay on the opposite side of the crowd from him all night.

Ellis wraps him up in a bear hug, and I want to punch him for the halfhearted way he hugs her back. If he upsets her tonight, I'll swear I'll—

"Happy birthday, son." My mom is standing in front of me with Ellis's parents right next to her.

"Thanks. Um, thank y'all for coming. I'm still a little shocked you're all here."

"So are we," Gary French says. "But when our daughter and daughter-in-law get something in their head, we're apparently obligated to go along with them."

Nora slaps his forearm. "What he's trying to say is that we wouldn't have missed it."

"How was your flight?"

That's the opening he needs. Gary is off and running, explaining why they hit turbulence in a way that only someone with his in-depth knowledge of atmospheric pressure could.

I look at the glass in Mom's hand, wonder how many she's had, and send up a prayer that she didn't bring anyone with her. She never picks winners, but her most recent choice is the jackpot of losers.

"You came all the way to Vegas alone just to celebrate my birthday?"

"Well, it's an important one," she says.

Every one she missed in the past was important to me.

"But I didn't fly out here alone."

My stomach knots.

"Gary booked us all on the same flight."

Relief floods my body. I wonder if he paid for Mom's airfare, too. It was either Ellis or her parents because my mom wouldn't have had the money to book a spontaneous flight.

Emil waves me over.

Nico's here, too. "How did she know how to get in touch with you?"

"Your girlfriend had a network going. She was determined to get a crowd here."

"She's a force to be reckoned with when she's determined."

"Yeah, she's also out of your league. You better do whatever that woman wants."

"Thanks a lot, you cruel bastard."

"Eh, consider my wisdom your birthday present."

"I'm touched. Next year, how about a free month's rent on the warehouse instead?"

"Dream on, my friend."

I continue to make my way through the guests. Some people are here for both of us. Old friends. Current mutuals. When Brody and I find ourselves cornered in the same group, we plaster on smiles and avoid eye contact.

How long are we going to do this, I wonder. He's going to have to come to terms with it at some point.

Even with the tension between us, this is a pretty incredible thing Ellis and Amanda did. Their intentions were pure, and it couldn't have been easy to wrangle all these people and keep it a secret.

I'm going to make the most of it, Brody be damned. Everyone else is enjoying the party. I may as well do the same.

I stand at a table in the corner and watch Ellis mingle for a while. She is having the time of her life. It's going to be a good night.

Our parents are all three still hanging out together. I make my way over to them to be sure Mom's doing okay. She seems surprisingly fine. I appreciate the Frenches being kind to her, especially Nora because I know how frustrated she used to get with her when I was growing up. It was hard for a mom like her to understand mine.

I leave them again and go to the bar to get Ellis a drink. When I see the yellow and red label on the backbar, I say, "Extra cherries."

The bartender adds one extra cherry. I wave my credit card at him. "More."

When her drink is ready, I find her talking to our parents.

"Are those my favorite cherries?"

"They are."

She takes the drink, and then she kisses me on the lips in a very not-sisterly kind of way.

"Ellis!" Nora's voice is high-pitched, shot through with shock at her daughter's response.

"Oh, right," Ellis says. "You guys didn't know about this yet. Well, now you do!" She shrugs and takes a sip of her drink. "Malcolm and I are together."

Her dad slams his glass onto the table. "The hell you are!" He turns his ire to me. "I've treated you like a son!"

"Well," Ellis says with a giggle that I wish she would've held inside. "I'm not treating him like a brother these days."

Not helpful, Buttercup.

"Ellis!" her mother's voice goes higher. "What is wrong with you?"

Now my mom squares her shoulders and faces Nora. "What is that supposed to mean? Is my son not good enough for your daughter?"

"Mom, please stop."

"No. I want to know what she meant by that."

Nora looks like she's on the verge of hyperventilating. Gary looks like his head might explode.

Mom keeps going. "For all I know, your daughter is only after my son's money."

"I'll have you know my daughter makes her own money," Gary says. "She works damn hard, and she doesn't need any man to take care of her."

Ellis looks at her dad like she can't believe her ears.

Her mom follows with, "That's right. Our daughter is a successful, talented young woman."

"And my son is a successful, talented man. I didn't raise him to be taken advantage of."

"Who raised him?" Nora eyes narrow at my mother. "We raised him more than you ever did!"

Ellis retreats.

I do the same, not wanting to get too far from her.

We keep going until our backs are against a wall, but we're right next to each other.

Our parents continue to argue. The party carries on around them. Oblivious.

Brody is the only other person who notices what's happening. For a moment, I think he's coming over to help, but he turns and heads toward the bathroom instead.

No one is coming to save us. It's just me and her.

A Mermaid Beckons
Ellis

"HELL OF A PARTY, huh? My brother's not speaking to us, and our parents are screaming at each other." I throw my hands in the air. "Please say something to keep me from crying."

"An olive oil broker and a mermaid walk into a wedding chapel."

"Okay. What's the punch line?"

"What if there isn't one? What if it's not a joke?"

"You can't be serious."

"I am."

"This dress really does make you stupid."

"I would marry you in jeans or in a mermaid tail and wings or in nothing at all. I don't care what you're wearing."

"We can't just get married, Malcolm."

"We're in Vegas. People just get married in this town every day. Our friends are all here, and our parents are already pissed off."

"If we turn Brody's thirtieth birthday party into our wedding reception, he will never forgive either one of us."

"Yeah, he will. He'll get over it, Ellis. They all will. You're supposed to go home from Vegas with a wild story to tell, and I can't think of anything wilder than the tale of how I captured a mermaid and made her my wife."

"Shut up and marry me."

We hold hands and run for the exit. We run and we don't stop until we reach The Marry Little Shipwreck. I appreciate the wordplay, but we choose it for the neon mermaid on the sign.

"We don't need a license?" I ask

Malcolm smiles. "Since when have we ever needed a license to make a rash decision?"

"Yeah, that's not really our style, is it?"

He opens the door to the chapel, and I step confidently onto the turquoise shag carpet, knowing I will never regret what we're about to do.

A woman wearing a coconut bra and a grass skirt shows us where to sign, and then she stamps a sea turtle on our hands to prove we've completed the necessary paperwork and paid our fee.

With Anne Bonny as our witness and Calico Jack officiating, we say, "I do." When the infamous pirate pronounces us man and wife by the power vested in him by Davy Jones, the foul-mouthed parrot on his shoulder says, "Free to fuck. Free to fuck."

We all take a shot of cheap rum, and the woman who stamped our hands points to a rack on the wall and tells me I can pick whichever sash I want. I choose a dark green one to match my dress, and position it across my body to be sure the words *Wedded Wench* are on full display.

Malcolm is given a drawstring bag filled with plastic beads, chocolate poker chips, and buffet coupons.

My husband takes my hand and hails a pedicab. Back at the hotel, everyone has calmed down. They've had time to have a few more drinks, which may or may not be a good thing. This party is about to get one more surprise.

Brody's eyes widen as they scan my torso. "That sash better be a fucking joke."

"Watch how you speak to my wife." Malcolm steps closer to me. "Remember when we used to tell people we were brothers? Well, funny story."

Amanda squeals. Maren squeals louder. Malcolm's Mom gasps. Dad shakes his head in disbelief. My Mom bursts into tears.

Brody steps toe-to-toe with Malcolm and says, "Did you really just marry my sister?"

Malcolm holds up his sheer black bag of booty. "She came with loot."

"Are those poker chips?"

"Pretty sure they're candy."

"Buy me a drink, asshole."

"I just got married. I think you're supposed to buy me a drink."

"I'm letting you live. You're buying the drinks."

"I'll buy the first round."

"You're buying all night long."

I push against their chests to separate them. "Uh, hello? It's my wedding night. He won't be drinking with you all night long."

Dad pulls me back. "I'll buy the goddamn drinks."

He jerks his chin toward Mom. "You go fix your mother."

Maren links her arm in mine, and Amanda brings Malcolm's mother over. We all go to Mom, who is drying her eyes with a drink napkin.

"Well," she says. "I should've known becoming a mermaid wouldn't be the craziest stunt you'd ever pull."

Becoming a mermaid.

I fish my phone out of my purse. No text. No email. It's seven o'clock here, but only five in Houston. Maybe, just maybe . . . my phone rings in my hand as if I've willed it to happen. I turn the screen toward Maren. "I can't look. Who is this?"

"It's Sedona Rain."

"Are you sure?"

"Answer your phone!"

"Hello."

"Have you been sitting on pins and needles waiting for our call?"

"Surprisingly, I've actually managed to keep myself pretty well occupied today. But I'm really glad to hear your voice. Does this mean . . .?"

"You're in. Welcome to the Fantasia Faeries, Ellisandra."

"Thank you!" Nothing could hold back my tears now.

I meet Malcolm's eyes across the room and give him a thumbs up. Maren and Amanda mob me before I can see his reaction.

The next voice I hear is Malcolm's mom saying, "What the hell is my son doing on that table?"

We all turn to see Malcolm, indeed standing on a table with his glass raised. "Guess what, Vegas?"

The whole bar yells, "What?"

"My wife just became a fairy mermaid!"

Everyone in here cheers like they actually know what the hell he's talking about.

Maren rests her head on my shoulder. "You married a maniac."

"I know. Isn't he great? Someday I might marry him for real."

"What?" Her head pops up. "You're not really—"

I flip the sash so only she can see the alternate message on the other side:

Wedded for the Weekend

"Shh. It's fun to have a secret."

Epilogue
Exactly One Year Later

Malcolm

"I can't believe I'm helping my wife hang her tail in the shower of an Italian villa."

It's more the "my wife" part than the tail hanging that I can't believe is actually happening.

"You're the one who said I could bring it."

"As if you were waiting on permission."

"True. But I asked, anyway. Out of courtesy."

"How'd I get lucky enough to have such a courteous wife?"

"When are you going to get tired of calling me your wife?"

"Never. It's still hard to believe it's real this time." I wrap my arms around her and pull her against my chest. All she's wearing is the towel she wrapped around her body after her shower. Her damp hair soaks through my t-shirt.

"Not everyone can get married on their existing wedding anniversary." She reaches up and playfully tugs on my beard.

I squeeze her tighter. Hard to imagine it was a year ago tonight when we ran out of a party in Vegas, got fake married, and let everyone believe it was real for over a month.

By the time we came clean, neither Ellis's brother or her dad had anything left to be shocked or upset about. We were dating, and that was that.

At least we weren't married. Neither of them said it, but I could read it on her dad's face.

Sometimes I wonder how long we'd have let them keep believing we were married if people hadn't started to question why we weren't moving in together. It was too soon in our relationship to live together. That wasn't even on our radar yet.

So, we realized the time had come to let them all in on the ruse.

There was some shock, a little grumbling, and a whole lot of relief. Not from me, though. I never said it out loud, but there was a part of me that always wished our secret had been real.

Five months later, I bought a house, and Ellis moved right in. At my request. Multiple requests, if I'm being honest, but once she finally agreed, she made it a home. A home with more mermaids than I'd have ever guessed would be watching me eat, shout at a game on the TV, work, and sleep. They're literally in every room.

And here we are now: six more months have passed, and we've eloped for the second time. But now, it's legal. She's my wife. My beautiful fairy mermaid wife.

"How long should we wait before we tell them?" she asks, making me laugh.

We won't wait so long this time, but it's nice to share a secret with her again for a little while. There is a knock at the door, and my heartbeat quickens. "Come on. I have a surprise for you."

"You got me a miniature Scottish Highland cow as a wedding present?"

Two attendants bring in the champagne and chocolate cake I've ordered, and I direct them to set it up on the table. The cork is popped, two glasses poured, and two slices plated with fresh strawberries before they leave. After they've gone, I set the black velvet box from the jeweler between our cake plates.

"That's not a mini cow," she says with a dramatic sigh.

"Keen eye, Buttercup. That is your one-year anniversary present. You've officially been a Fantasia Faerie for a year."

"I didn't even think about our wedding anniversary being the same day as my Fantasia Faerie anniversary. Yes! Past me was a visionary. Double presents forever."

"I might not always get you a present for your mermaid anniversary."

"Too late. You started a tradition, and you know how much I love traditions."

"Right. Being that you're so traditional and all." I love the way she can twist any situation to suit her own whimsical outlook. I am not ever buying her a miniature Scottish Highland cow, though. But I guess I'll be buying two anniversary gifts for the rest of our lives. I can live with that.

"Open it." My first idea was a gold mermaid with emeralds in the tail or maybe wings with emeralds. The jeweler basically told me he didn't do tacky. He said it nicely, but I got the message. There's a reason I deal in olive oil and not jewelry. Besides, she already has several mermaid necklaces. This one needed to be special.

Her elegant fingers lift the lid, and her eyes go wide when she sees the emerald necklace. It's a simple design, but it has a wow factor. A large solitaire set in the center of a platinum jasmine flower. It's the source of that sweet, slightly fruity, and lightly peppery scent of her shampoo I always loved, but could never place until I read the bottle and did a little research.

I'm not sure if she'll recognize the flower or understand why I chose it, but as long as she loves it, that's all that matters.

"Malcolm, this is so beautiful. I can't believe you got me an emerald."

"Of course I did. Green is your signature color."

"Shut up and fuck me."

Ellis

I drop my towel in front of my husband in the bedroom of our private villa overlooking Lake Como, and I pause, thinking how much my life resembles a movie in this moment, how there was a time when this would have felt like a fantasy.

Tomorrow, we will drive for hours to tour olive orchards and a mill, so I can experience the romance of olive oil for myself. He wants to show me how and why he fell in love with it, but I already know. I get it.

What I may never understand is how we fell so deeply in love with each other. None of this was ever supposed to happen, or maybe it was meant to be all along. I still spend a lot of time wondering which is true. I think I might always wonder. And I think that's okay.

After all, what's life without wonder?

He sits on the edge of the bed and pats his lap, intending for me to lay across it. I don't have any stress or anxiety to escape tonight, but my senses crave the sting of his hand, nonetheless. How deep does the well of bliss go when you're already so relaxed?

"I've never been spanked on foreign soil." I twirl a section of hair as I walk toward him.

"Of all the things I've done in Italy, I've never spanked anyone's wife here."

"Well, clearly, that makes us equals in this moment."

"No, Buttercup, we're not equals." He reaches for me, and his mouth tilts, equal parts grin and smirk. "Your ass belongs to me right now."

Damn, I love my husband.

I lay across his lap, and his big hand massages my sore glutes. It's easy to lose track of time swimming in Lake Como, with or without a tail. That water is a balm for a weary mermaid. I love performing, but sometimes, I don't realize how depleted I am.

Malcolm refills my well in so many ways, and now he's brought me to Italy, this country he loves so dearly, and he's introducing me to all his favorite places. But the Lake Como portion of our trip has been solely for me.

He knew. He always knows what I need before I do.

The first slap stings like it does every time, and I squirm on his lap—not trying to get away from him by any means, but it awakens a buzzing under my skin, endorphins like bees that rush through my veins.

And then, he tames them. They settle, but leave warm honey flowing through me as he rubs over my muscles, masking the pink welts of his handprint that I know are rising. His gentle groan tells me they are there.

When two of his thick fingers slide through my seam, I moan. I'm sure he knew exactly the reaction his fingers would elicit before he ever touched me there. We are familiar to each other in every way, but even though we sometimes fall into a certain choreography, nothing feels routine.

Or maybe it does, and maybe that's exactly why it feels so right.

He stands and takes me with him, flipping me onto my back so he can cradle my body in his arms before he tosses me onto the bed. I know I'm about to be airborne, but my stomach still flutters when he lets me go.

I roll onto my side to watch him undress. My thighs instinctively rub together when he climbs onto the bed next to me. His hand slides between them.

He kisses me softly and says, "Lie back."

"No." I push against his chest. "You can go first tonight. I want to be on top."

As soon as I straddle him, he grips my hips and pulls them all the way to his chest, totally bypassing his dick before I have a chance to line it up at my opening. My shins press into the mattress to hold me upright.

"Oh, you can definitely be on top." He smiles, but his eyes are laser-focused on my pussy grazing his chest. "On top of my mouth."

"I don't always have to get mine first." We've had this conversation before, and I know he's unlikely to agree with me tonight, but I definitely don't mind when he gets off before me. Probably because it happens so rarely, but I'd like to think I'd feel the same way if it were a more even split. I like to think I'm not so spoiled, even as I'm enjoying the spoiling.

"You absolutely need to get yours first. Usually." He makes eye contact long enough to wink at me before his gaze falls again. "Bring that pretty pussy to my mouth, princess."

"So, if there are passenger princesses and travel princesses, what does this make me?" I tease as I begin the awkward repositioning.

"The queen. Shut up and sit on my face."

Malcolm

I've dragged Ellis through three different orchards and a mill. She's patiently listened to me talk shop with everyone, and smiled every time I introduced her as my wife. I've watched her eyes as she took in all the knowledge being shared with her.

She genuinely paid attention to everyone, from the orchard workers to the master miller. It's who she is, and part of why I love her so damn much.

Tonight is the last night of our secret honeymoon. This restaurant is quaint, tucked away, and it's the perfect place to enjoy good wine and exquisite oil after such a long day.

"We leave tomorrow," I remind her. "We should probably come up with a plan for telling everyone that we are officially married."

"Lean over here. Bring your wine."

I do as she's asked and lean in for the selfie. She makes sure her ring is prominent in the shot. Immediately after taking it, she starts typing.

"You can't post that anywhere yet," I say, sitting back up in my chair. "Your ring is on full display."

"I didn't post it on social media," she assures me, dropping her phone into her purse.

I know Maren already knows, so I assume she was sending it to her. "Okay. Good."

"I started a new family text."

The sip of wine I've just taken suddenly feels heavy on my tongue. I swallow hard. "You didn't send them that picture, did you?"

My phone buzzes in my pocket, and I know the answer. Of course she did.

"We had a problem. We needed a simple solution. I solved it."

She pops an olive into her mouth and smiles, as if telling her parents she's married via text is totally acceptable. Actually, with Ellis, they probably won't be surprised in the least. Her dad will roll his eyes. Her mom will clench her jaw. Brody will sigh and shake his head, but then he'll laugh. I'm sure that's who is buzzing my phone.

"Um, you didn't include my mom in that group text, did you?"

"I told you it was for the family. She's family, so, what do you think?"

"We're going to have to stay here for another week. At least."

"Relax. It'll be fine. She likes me now."

That much is true. Mom does like her. Not sure she's going to be any more excited about this marriage announcement than she was our first one, though. What's done is done, I guess. I reach for the wine bottle.

Ellis holds up an olive, her hand pulling back and rocking, preparing to toss it at my face. I open my mouth, and for the first time ever, she actually hits her target instead of bouncing food off my forehead.

The pungent olive juice trickles to the hinge of my jaw, locking it for a moment.

She lifts her wine glass. "To Italy."

I lift mine. "To new traditions."

"You think Italy is going to become a tradition for us?"

"I think you making spontaneous decisions is a tradition."

"I don't think a tradition can be spontaneous."

"Not for most people, no. But you are not most people, Buttercup."

"True. I mean, how many of your friends have mermaids for wives?"

"I can honestly say I am the only person I know who is married to a mermaid."

"You're welcome."

I take an olive and aim for her mouth. It bounces off her nose. Her head falls back as she laughs. The emerald around her neck shines in the lights strung through the trees. My phone buzzes again, and I ignore it entirely.

Ellis

As soon as our plane lands, Maren's warning text shows up.

> Your welcome party is waiting at baggage claim. There are balloons.

> Who all is here?

> Everyone from your new group text. Congratulations.

> I guess we can survive a public display with balloons.

> There's cake at your parents' house. And food. There was a band setting up in the backyard when we left.

> Tell me you're joking.

> Your mom and your mother-in-law said you're not the only one who can pull off a surprise. So, welcome home. Hope you enjoy your surprise wedding reception.

I glance over at Malcolm and wonder if I should tell him about this.

We are not dressed for a wedding reception, or any other type of party. Looks like we're celebrating in our travel clothes. At least we'll be physically comfortable.

***

There is a string quartet in the backyard, along with all our friends. A full buffet in the dining room. And a gift table. Our mothers had one day of notice. They certainly made the most of it.

Malcolm comes inside and finds me staring at the cake. "It's a lot to come home to," he says. "But we are lucky to be so loved."

"I know. I just never thought our mothers would end up being coconspirators."

"Well, you know what they say about having a common enemy."

"I'm not their enemy."

"Not you. Just your . . . spontaneity."

"Well, that's not changing."

"I hope not."

"Wanna cut the cake?"

"Oh, sure. Implicate me in your crime." He takes the knife I'm offering and commits the sin of cutting the cake with no mom present to take a picture. "You want to get a shot of this, so they'll at least have a photo?"

I shrug, but I take the picture. And then I carry the ganache-covered evidence of my brazenness into the backyard.

Malcolm has dozens of pictures from Italy on his phone, and our family is eager to see them all. They don't even notice the plate in my hand. I escape the huddle and stand next to the pool to eat my cake in peace.

Quick movement in my peripheral vision draws my attention, but it's too late. My plate goes flying as we crash into the deep end.

We come up sputtering and spitting.

"You just had to do it, didn't you?"

"I mean, come on. The way you were standing there, looking all provocative in your leggings and my shirt, swallowing half your body . . . Clearly, I had no choice."

"Ellis Danielle Freeeeeeench!" My mother's voice drowns out the music. "You cut the cake? How could you? I swear sometimes, you—"

A slice of waterlogged chocolate cake floats past as my husband pushes me under.

I pull him with me, and our underwater smiles say it all.

We're in this together. Coconspirators to the end.

Thank you for reading!

Also from INDIE SPARKS

Steamy Rom-Com Duologies:

VENGEFUL VIXENS:
Your Boss Says Hi!

She's only looking for a rebound guy, but her ex's boss plays for keeps. He's a former NFL player who used to have thousands of women screaming his name every week. Now, he only wants one woman to scream his name, and she just might become his biggest fan yet.

Your Trainer Says Hi!

She only wants to see her ex's beloved personal trainer in the gym—until he convinces her his hot tub could do wonders for her aching muscles. He isn't wrong, but between the heat, the bubbles, and his off-the-clock skills, she might be in too deep before she knows it. He's definitely not her type. So, why can't she stop seeing him?

NAUGHTY AT THE NOUVEAU:
Maintenance & Management

She's the new property manager. He's the new maintenance supervisor. They rub each other the wrong way . . . until they start to rub each other so very right. There's a non-fraternization policy, so they really shouldn't. But there's only one bed!

Landscaping & Leasing

He ghosted her after an unfortunate incident that she had absolutely no control over—and now, she's accidentally hired his landscaping company. She may not be completely immune to his charms (that voice!), but she's not weak enough to fall for him twice. But what if she doesn't know the whole story about why he disappeared from her life?

Small Town Second Chance Romance:

Peri

They were the wildest couple in town once, but that was a long time ago. They're not restless small-town kids anymore. And she's not back in town to see him. But seeing him once won't hurt anything. How much trouble could they get into as adults? Hardly any if you disregard the dirty karaoke and the lewd (allegedly) graffiti . . . and that old flame reigniting like an inferno.

IVYDELL, a Steamy Novella Series:

Ivy Dell takes Ivydell!

Ivy Dell McAdams is grieving the loss of her grandmother. Gran
was her favorite person in the world. And Gran's favorite place
was a fabled, mystical west Texas town called Ivydell. She loved
the place so much, she convinced Ivy's mother to name her after
it.

Gran's stories always sounded like fairytales, but Ivy's restless
and sad, a terrible combination. What better way to shake up
her life than to take a little hiatus to middle-of-nowhere Ivydell?

The way Gran described the place, Ivy half expects to find Stars
Hollow meets 1980s Marfa meets Lily Dale, NY. It turns out
her farcical guess is not far off . . .

But more goes on in Ivydell than Ivy Dell could've imagined. It's
truly got that magical quality that Gran waxed poetic about all
those years.

And it just might have the perfect magical man for her grand-
daughter. Or maybe he's a jerk who just happens to be good
with his hands. Of course, he could be the one. But he's probably not.
After all, love in Ivydell? Pfft, they can't even get highspeed
internet!
Where the Hell is Ivy Dell?

Shit Happens in Ivydell
Who Pissed Off Ivy Dell?
Bitch, Please! It's Ivydell

www.ingramcontent.com/pod-product-compliance
Lightning Source LLC
Chambersburg PA
CBHW021416110726
47901CB00008B/2187